CYNTHIA HICKEY

Caper Goes Missing

A Tiny House Mystery, Book Two

By Cynthia Hickey

DEDICATION

Thank you to all my readers who eagerly await the
next frolicking adventure.

Chapter One

"Robinson wants to take a vacation," Eric Drake, the area's handsome park ranger, told me as we sat outside my house on an early summer morning. "He wants to know if you can handle watching over the campground for him. After the fiasco with the Campground Babysitter, he doesn't trust many people."

"I guess so. Summer's here and my rentals are filling up. I'm sure the campground will be the same." It might very well be more than I could handle. "How long will he be gone?"

"A month." Eric laughed at my shocked expression. "I'll help as much as I can, sweet Clarice Josephine Turley. The parks around here will be busy, too, with hikers and those who insist on primitive camping, but I can lend a hand. Just put a notice on the camp bulletin board that you can be contacted here. That will keep you from being spread too thin."

I couldn't help but remember the murder on the

other side of the lake just a little over a month ago. Maybe I wouldn't be reminded every time I drove past the spot, but knowing me, I'd avoid that particular site like it was haunted. "I can get Roy to help."

After his stepson, Danny, had stolen my laptop, I'd hired the man to do repairs around the tiny house community of Heavenly Acres and given them the largest of the small houses to move his family into. Danny and his mother, Tammy, also hired themselves out to do odd jobs when needed. It worked out well for everyone.

My attention returned to Lake Blue Waters. Here, a rich eccentric had built tiny houses and created a wonderful community. On the other side, he'd built a campground in one of the state's national parks. Together, it created a popular oasis with both short- and long-term residents. Even after getting embroiled in a murder mystery and almost being killed, I didn't regret for one moment accepting the job as overseer. I'd made some wonderful friends, and my life had purpose again. After so many years caring for Grams, I'd drifted after her death until accepting this position.

"It'll definitely be a challenge." I smiled at Eric. "But I'm up to it."

"I know you are, sweetheart." He leaned over and kissed me, something I'd never get tired of.

Caper, the spaniel pup I'd inherited upon Grams' death, leaned on my leg, pulling my attention away from the feel of Eric's lips on mine. I glanced down. "What's this? You're always bringing me things that make no sense." I removed a small leather pouch from her mouth.

"What is it?" Eric leaned over.

I opened the bag and gasped at the sight of what appeared to be several diamonds. "Where did you get this, Caper? You're a naughty girl." How in the world would I find who they belonged to? I couldn't very well go door-to-door alerting everyone that my dog was a thief.

"Missing diamonds were on the news last night." Eric took the bag from me. "I'll have to report this to Detective Davis. It's both unfortunate and a good thing that Caper likes shiny objects. I got the feeling from the news report that more were taken than what's in this pouch."

"True, but she couldn't have opened the bag and looked inside. Maybe the thief divided the loot." I swiped the pup's muddy footprints from my leg. "I'm guessing she's been nosing around the campground."

"Or someone's flower bed here." He narrowed his eyes. "Don't get involved, CJ."

"I don't intend to." I shuddered.

"Uh, huh." He slid his cell phone from a clip on his belt and called Davis. After he hung up, he said, "He's sending Milton and the new guy over."

"I hope the new cop is better than the old one." Officer Perk had turned out to be as dirty as my dog's muddy paws, he and his murderous girlfriend both.

By the time Milton arrived with a woman officer who appeared to be in her mid-thirties, I'd finished my second cup of coffee. "Officer Lowery, this is the local pain in the backside, CJ Turley, who also happens to be the overseer of this community."

The dark-haired officer smiled. "It's a pleasure to meet you. I heard all about your recent adventures. As far as I'm concerned, you did a great service to this community."

I liked her already and thrust out my hand. "Likewise."

Milton rolled his eyes. "I should have known you women would stick together. Where are the diamonds?"

"Right here." Eric pulled the pouch from his pocket. "CJ's dog found them."

"Too bad the little cutie can't tell us where she got them." Lowery leaned down and scratched behind Caper's ears. "Or can you, sweetie?"

A lick on her hand was the only answer.

"Whoever stole these rocks will be looking for them. We'll keep our eyes and ears open." Eric gave me a quick kiss on the forehead. "See you later. I'm off to make my rounds."

I nodded. I'd be heading over to talk to Robinson and make sure I was clear on my duties during his absence.

With the jewels now in their possession, Milton and Lowery returned to their squad car and drove away. "Come on, girl." I climbed into my new golf cart with bright red vinyl seats. The previous cart had been damaged by a tree when lightning struck, causing the tree to fall, almost crushing Caper and my neighbor, Mags. I set the dog on the seat next to me and headed for the trailer Robinson lived in. Since he was loading up the back of his camper, it appeared my duties were starting immediately.

"Howdy." He glanced over and shut the door. "Since you're here, I'm guessing you agreed to watch over this place?"

"I did. Can you fill me in on what exactly you do?"

"I rent the sites, monitor the area, make sure it's kept clean including the bathrooms, collect the fees beforehand, mind you…and return the deposit if the site is left as found."

"Do you monitor who you rent to?"

He shook his head. "As long as they pay, they're in. If there are too many complaints about noise, we alert the ranger, and he gives them the boot." He handed me a folded sheet of paper and a key ring "Everything is done online. Here is the login information. Any key you can possibly need is on this ring."

"Looks easy enough." I slipped the paper into the pocket of my denim capris. "Where you headed?"

"Across country to Colorado to see my brother. It's been a while." He smiled. "I'm leaving the place in your capable hands." With a jaunty salute, he climbed into the driver's seat of his truck and left me in charge.

I did a leisurely drive around the campgrounds before heading back to the other side of the lake. Everything looked peaceful all the way around. Spotting Mags, my dear friend and neighborhood busybody, I stopped next to her flower garden. "Guess who's in charge of the campgrounds for the next month."

She straightened and pulled off her garden

gloves. "What happened to the handsome man who runs the place?"

"Vacation."

"Pooh. I wanted to get to know him better." She frowned. "Time is of the essence. I'm not getting any younger."

I laughed. "Here's some news to take your mind off your heartbreak." I told her about Caper finding the diamonds.

Her face lit up. "Yay, another mystery to immerse ourselves in."

"No, thank you. Not after what happened the last time."

"Don't be a limp waistband. This isn't a murder. Put your big-girl panties on. What's our first clue?"

Shaking my head, I said, "Caper's paws were muddy."

"Hmm." She tapped her forefinger against her chin. "That isn't much to go on."

Since I figured this was one mystery that would be impossible for us to solve, I decided to indulge her fantasy. "They had to have been buried here at camp, or around the lake."

"CJ., That's acres of possibilities."

"Maybe this is one we should leave to the authorities."

"Don't be silly. That Milton is a dunderhead, and Davis is way too busy."

"There's a new officer who seems okay. A woman."

"Good. She'll see things our way." She rubbed her hands together. "Yesterday before time to open, two people wearing those silly animal heads broke into the jewelry store and stole the diamonds. Today your dog digs them up. This tells me—" she held up a finger, "the culprit is close."

Wasn't that what I'd already determined? "As you said, it's a lot of ground to cover."

"Then, we'd best get started. Any new renters?"

"Mags, the place is full to capacity. Where have you been?"

"Head deep in hydrangeas, dear. They need to be babied, you know."

"So, now you want to drive aimlessly on the off chance we see something?" My eyes widened.

"As good an idea as any." She climbed into the cart, placing Caper on her lap.

I needed to make the rounds anyway to make sure all the new renters were settled in. Twenty-seven houses in all, twenty-seven full. My home was part of my salary, as was Roy's. Five more were owned and only the plot rented, which left fifteen for me to monitor. I'd been warned summers were busy, but I hadn't counted on fifty campsites in addition to my regular duties.

"You're awfully quiet."

I glanced at Mags. "Just wondering how I'm going to get it all done. Mind if we stop at the Olson place first?"

"You're driving."

Roy sat outside eating what looked like a breakfast burrito and glanced up as we stopped. "I was going to come by in a bit and get my jobs for today."

"Not a problem." I hopped from the cart and joined him at the table. "I'm watching over the camp for about a month and can really use your help. Tammy's too, if she doesn't mind keeping up with the restrooms."

He wiped his mouth with a napkin. "I reckon I can drive through there once or twice a day and see what needs doing. I don't have to empty the septic, do I? That place where the motor homes dump their—" He paled.

"I…uh…isn't there a company that does that?"

"I hope so." He set down the uneaten portion of his breakfast. "Since it's summer, I can have Danny work on keeping the weeds to a minimum. The grass around the lake is getting tall. Snakes will love that."

"That is a great idea. I saw a riding mower near Mr. Robinson's trailer." Maybe I could scrape up a bit of money to pay Danny for his summer job. If there was a mystery here, another pair of eyes would be beneficial, not that I planned on getting involved.

Chapter Two

While I drank my coffee the next morning, I pulled up the website to the campground and checked to see whether any newcomers were due to arrive. Two. That meant I'd have to check the sites to make sure they were ready for check-in. It would be the perfect opportunity to get more acquainted with the property on the other side of the lake.

"Where's Eric?" Mags sat across from me, a thermos in one hand.

"Working. Good morning to you, too." I smiled.

"Good. What are we up to today?" She held the thermos out. "Fortification for whatever lies ahead."

"Wine or coffee?" I raised an eyebrow.

"You know that loose granddaughter of mine is the wine drinker."

When I'd first taken the overseer job, Mags had called the resident of number four a harlot. Imagine my surprise when I discovered Amber was her granddaughter. "I thought you two got along now."

"She's dating Davis." Her lip curled.

I straightened, closing my laptop. "Really? I did not see that coming."

"Why not? The detective is a handsome man, and Amber has always had an eye for a good-looking male."

I could say the same about Mags, but wisely kept my mouth shut. She'd set her sights on Mr. Robinson, poor man. It was probably a good thing he'd decided to take a vacation. "I've got to head over and check out a couple of campsites, then check on the new tenants here. That's my agenda for the day."

"We're not going to look for the diamond thief?" Her face fell.

"It's not at the top of my priority list, Mags. I almost died chasing after Addie Morris."

"But wasn't it thrilling?" She clasped her hands together. "I have little excitement in my life. Who knows how much time I have left to enjoy any sort of adventure?" She tilted her head and batted her eyelashes.

"Don't try to manipulate me with guilt. It wasn't you that almost drowned in the mud or got chased at gunpoint." I closed my eyes against the memory. I might have helped catch a murderer, but I was nothing more than a coward—certainly not cut out to be an amateur sleuth.

"Fine. I'm taking my coffee home to putter among my flowers." She marched away, leaving me feeling like a jerk.

"Come on, Caper. Let's get to work." I glanced around, expecting to see my dog sniffing around the immediate area. If she was going to continue wandering off, I'd have to put a leash on her. The look of betrayal I'd see in her big dark eyes would wound me. "Caper."

Sighing, I climbed into the golf cart and headed for the campground. As I got closer, I recognized the shrill yip of the excited spaniel. Definitely need to put a leash on her. I followed the sound, only to have it disappear when I reached the entrance to the campground. I called her name again to no response. She'd show up. She always did.

I tacked my contact information to the camp bulletin board, then tried several keys on the riding lawnmower until I located the small tarnished gold one that fit. Voilà. I'd have Roy fill it with gas and get Danny started on his summer job. Things were going smoothly. How hard could running both places be?

Feeling optimistic, I resumed my drive through the campsites, stopping at the two empty ones being rented later that day. A yawning hole in the fire pit had me out of the cart and grabbing a shovel from the back of it to scoop dirt and ash back in place. The rest of the site looked clean and ready.

The lake shimmered in the morning sun. A lone orange canoe floated on the water. Someone would be unhappy it had come loose from its mooring. Just as I started to turn back to the cart, I heard Caper's bark. Her head popped over the edge of the canoe.

What in the world? My heart leaped in my throat at the thought of having to go after her. Water was not my friend. I had no idea how to row a boat and didn't like swimming, at least not lately. I radioed Eric for help.

"I'm too far away, sweetheart. You'll have to swim out to her."

"I hate the water."

"Can you swim?"

"Yes, very well, in fact, but after almost drowning during the whole Addie Morris thing, I'd rather not get my face wet."

"You were pinned under a tree. It isn't the same thing at all." He chuckled. "You take a shower, don't you? Think of the lake as a great big bathtub."

"Right." I hung up and contemplated my options, then called Roy.

"I'll send Danny right over. He's swum in that lake plenty of times."

"That's right." I remember him doing that very thing when we busted him for taking my laptop. In an attempt to get away, he'd jumped in and started swimming. I sat at the stone picnic table under a metal canopy and waited.

Rather than come to my side of the water, Danny dove in on his side and swam toward my yipping pup. The closer he got to her, the more excited her bark. How had she gotten into the canoe and out on the lake? It would be quite a feat for her to climb inside as she wasn't big, but my dog was persistent, if nothing else.

Danny pulled himself into the canoe and rowed to shore. I met him at the edge and took a squirming Caper in my arms. "Thank you very much."

He held up a pouch similar to the one Caper had found the day before. "It's empty, but I heard from Mags that diamonds were in one like this."

"Yes, they were." I took the pouch and set it in the back of the cart before handing the lawnmower key to Danny. "Here you go. Once it's full of gas, you're all set to keep the grounds mowed. I'll pay you one hundred dollars a week." I'd find money in the budget somewhere. "It's only for the month until Mr. Robinson returns."

He grinned. "That's great. If I do a good job, he might keep me on. I'm going to be a park ranger like Eric, so this is perfect." He raced for the mower.

I didn't see how mowing and being a park ranger related, but couldn't help but smile at the young man's enthusiasm. I set Caper in the cart. "You, my cutie, are going on a leash, but good job at finding another pouch." I patted her head and climbed in the cart, made a quick survey of the second campsite, then sped home to call Davis.

"Doesn't mean it belonged to the thief," he said.

"It's a good possibility. My dog seems to have a knack for finding stolen, shiny objects."

"Dogs also like to chew on leather."

I sighed. "Are you coming to get the pouch or not? I also want you to find out how my dog ended up in the middle of the lake."

"She climbed in the boat to take a nap and floated away. Be there in a few." Click.

Detective Davis could be the most infuriating man. I wished Amber all the luck in her relationship with him.

While I waited, I fetched a leash from inside the house and set to work making a line to attach it to so Caper could wander back and forth without

13

getting tangled. I'd seen a photo once of a wire stretched between two trees, and the leash looped on that. The dog moved the length of the wire with ease. "Wander off now, you little scamp." Pleased with myself, I rested my hands on my hips and surveyed my work.

Caper sat and stared up at me with soulful eyes. If she could talk, I bet she'd be telling me she couldn't find any more missing things while tied up.

"I agree, but I can't have anything happening to you. You don't have the run of the land, little girl."

"Are you expecting her to answer?" Davis stepped beside me.

"We have our way of communicating." I pulled the pouch from my pocket. "Sorry. It will have my fingerprints and Caper's teeth marks. Oh, and Danny's prints."

He rolled his eyes. "You don't make my job easier. The opposite, in fact."

I grinned. "I'm skilled in that area."

"Nothing to brag about." He turned and strode down the road toward Amber's house. He'd barely left me before Mags showed up.

"What happened?" She crossed her arms. "You went snooping without me?"

"No, I didn't." I told her of Caper's escapade.

"The dog did something good, and you reward her by tying her up? That doesn't seem right."

"She could have fallen out of the canoe and drowned. Caper needs to stay put where she belongs."

"What's with you and drowning?" Mags shook her head. "Finding the second pouch leads me to

14

believe the thief resided at the campsite. Maybe still does. Think. I'm sure you saw a clue."

I twisted my mouth. "I did fill in a hole in a fire pit that could have been dug up by Caper." Or any animal, actually. "It doesn't mean anything. I didn't see any dirt on the pouch."

"Cleaned off by the dog."

I shrugged, turning as a car approached. "This must be one of my new renters. I'll catch up with you later, okay?"

"Good. We can make plans when I return from my MRI on my knee." She bustled home, leaving me resigned to the fact she wasn't going to let go of wanting to find the diamond thief.

"Welcome to Heavenly Acres. I'm CJ Turley, the overseer." I smiled at the young couple in the car.

"Thanks," the man said. "I'm Mike Rowe and this is my wife, Kim. We're early but were hoping you'd be ready for us." He glanced over at Caper who ran up and down her line as if being chased.

"We're ready. Follow me." I climbed into the cart and led them to number ten, hoping they wouldn't be as evil as the previous tenant. A house couldn't be blamed for the sins of its resident. This wasn't a horror film.

After filling out the paperwork and going over the rules of our community, I handed them the keys. "Enjoy your stay."

"I think we will," Kim said, her smile seeming a bit forced. Maybe she was shy. Either way, I'd filled the last rental and couldn't squelch the sense of pride that rose in me.

I left the couple to get settled, moving to the side when a dark paneled van pulled alongside its temporary home. A middle-aged man got out and opened the back, revealing a lot of boxes. Since the rentals came furnished, it seemed like a lot of stuff for someone staying less than a month, but it wasn't any of my business. I tossed another smile toward the Rowes and drove off to "plan" with Mags.

She stood in the road watching the goings-on of number ten. "That's the kind of van that murderers use."

I rolled my eyes. "It's also the kind of van people use to move things." I climbed out of the cart. "Come on. Offer me that coffee again."

"I can't."

"Why not?"

"I poured it out in a snit. I'll make you some tea. I have a mystery of my own to solve at this time." She entered the house, leaving me with my mouth hanging open.

Chapter Three

I followed her into her cluttered home full of knickknacks and crocheted doilies. "What kind of mystery?"

She gave a sheepish grin. "I seem to have misplaced my favorite pair of…underpants."

If I'd had anything in my mouth, I'd have spewed it down the front of me. "Excuse me?"

"I fear I left them in the doctor's office."

I sat on the sofa, gently moving aside her cat. "Why do you think that? A person would know whether they put their panties back on."

"Well, I can't remember, and I'm not wearing them right now." She stomped the few feet to her kitchen.

Feeling a change of subject might be in order, I asked, "How's the knee?"

"Still sore. I might need a replacement, the doctor said. First, we're trying supplements." She pulled a pitcher of tea from her refrigerator, added some sort of juice into the glasses, then handed me one.

I took a cautious sip, my eyes widening. "Wow. What's in here?"

"Muscadine juice. Amber visited a winery yesterday and brought me back some. Delicious, isn't it?"

"Yum." I took a bigger drink. "I want some of this."

"You'll have to go get some. Have Eric take you. Make it a date."

I just might. While we'd shared a few kisses, and he ate supper with me most nights, we'd never gone on a proper date. Maybe a day of wine tasting would be perfect. "When Robinson returns, I rather like that idea."

Mags started rummaging through a basket next to the washer/dryer combo. "They're white, if that helps."

"Your underwear?" I don't think my brows could go any higher. "That's the most common color, Mags. Forget about them. Buy some new ones in a variety of cheerful colors."

"I liked those." She sighed. "Okay, let's focus on the more important mystery around here. The diamonds." She turned and pulled a brand-new purple clipboard from a drawer. An ink pen adorned with a peacock feather stuck through the clip. "You deserve something new to take notes on after your misadventure."

Touched, I lifted the glass to my lips to keep tears from forming. "You're sweeter than you like people to know."

"Keep my secret, will you?"

"Absolutely." Resigned to digging into yet another mystery that could put me in danger, I set my glass on a sandstone coaster on the coffee table and took the clipboard. "We know nothing."

"Diamonds were stolen and possibly divided. Write that down." She sat across from me. "Which means there are more diamonds out there waiting to be found. Point number two…the thief is close by, just like last time."

"That's what I'm afraid of," I muttered, writing on the page in front of me.

"Don't forget someone sent your dog out to sea, so to speak."

I jerked my head up. "That's right. Too much of a coincidence for her to be in possession of a leather pouch for the second time, then pushed from shore in a canoe." Someone had it out for my dog. A new resolve rose. I'd find out who wanted to hurt sweet little Caper. "All right, let's do this."

"Wonderful." Mags clapped. "Where do we start?"

"How about a slow drive around the campground looking for actual clues, then the tiny house community. We'll focus on anyone who's checked in the last few days. Those are our primary suspects." Which would be most of the campers, but it was a start. Since it was nearing lunchtime, we had all afternoon to take a ride.

Mags pushed to her feet and reached for my glass. I slapped her hand away. "I'm not finished, and it's too good to waste."

"I'll pour it into a travel mug, silly. I'm going to make sandwiches. We might be gone a while." She snatched the glass and bustled to the counter.

I stepped outside to wait and surveyed all I was responsible for. It being summer, children played in the community park. A few residents walked their dogs. A peaceful place to spend some time, one would think. Yet, since my arrival, we'd had burglaries and murder. Something rotten lurked behind the calm façade. I prayed it wouldn't become the norm.

"Ready." Mags rushed past me. "We need to fetch the dog. She seems to be quite the snooper."

Caper was more than happy to be let off her leash and settled on the seat between us. Tail wagging, she stared straight ahead as we circled the lake.

The sound of the lawn mower, laughter, and the splashing of swimmers greeted us. Instead of mowing, Danny sat on the equipment and flirted with a pretty young girl in a bright yellow bikini. I beeped my horn and sent him back to work. I wasn't paying him to spend time with the campers. He could do that after he finished his job.

I stopped at the end of the road that wound around the campsites, trying to decide which way to go. It didn't matter, really. We'd canvass them all.

"When in doubt, go right," Mags said.

So I did. I looked from side to side for anything out of place. What did a jewel thief look like? Addie hadn't looked like a thief and murderer. Neither had the previous overseer who'd had her share in the crime. Former Officer Perks, seemingly friendly and good-looking, hadn't fit the profile either. Any one of these campers could be the person we looked for. Even the gray-haired woman striding along the side of the road.

Caper barked.

The woman startled, jumped to the side, and fell into a bush.

I stopped the cart and rushed to her aid. "I'm so sorry. Are you alright?"

"That dog is a nuisance." She declined my offer to help her and brushed leaves from her cotton walking shorts. "Always running around here barking and begging for table scraps. Isn't there a leash law?"

"Yes, but there's no harm when she's in my cart." I scowled. "If she's been a problem, you should have come to me. I'm the temporary one in charge. My information is on the bulletin board."

"I'm here on a peaceful retreat with some of my girlfriends. We aren't here to read the board." She strode away, arms pumping at her sides.

"That's one rude woman," Mags said. "You should have gotten her name. She doesn't like your dog, which means she could be the one who pushed her into the lake."

"That's quite a stretch." I resumed my seat in the cart, but decided to see which site she went to, then get her name from the reservations.

The woman glared at us, then entered a camper at site 101. Two other women glanced up at us with curiosity.

I introduced myself and asked whether they had any issues I could help them with.

"No." A woman with dyed hair the color of a pineapple glanced at her friend whose long gray hair fell down her back. A beaded, leather headband held the long tresses away from her face. "Myrna?"

"Not a thing." The aging hipster smiled. "Things couldn't be better. I'm Myrna Flutter, by the way. This is Carol Moore. The sourpuss inside is Ioda Warren. We've been friends since grade school."

"That's marvelous. My friend here is Mags Snyder. Please let me know if you need anything at all. I'll do my best to take care of whatever it is." My cell phone rang, sending the musical notes to "Chitty Chitty Bang Bang" into the air. I glanced at the screen. Spam.

Satisfied the two women would take care of their angry friend, I climbed back into the cart and continued our slow drive. A few sites away, two young men in their thirties raised beer cans to us in a toast. I hoped they wouldn't be a problem come curfew.

Mags tapped my arm. "Stop here. See that man? I've seen him before."

I studied the tall man with salt-and-pepper hair who lounged in a chair at site 107, cigarette in one hand, and stared out over the lake. "Maybe he's camped here before?"

"Until you came along, I never came over here."

"In town?"

She shrugged. "Maybe, but I usually have my things delivered."

True. Mags was a homebody for sure. "I still don't see the problem."

"My gut tells me….something."

The man turned, caught sight of us, and grinned.

"Mags Snyder. It's been a long time." He unfolded from his chair, tossed the cigarette into the fire pit, and came toward us.

"Oh, yes. Frank Dickson. He built the house I used to live in." She lowered her voice. "Never did like the guy."

Caper started barking, making it difficult for the man to say anything. He stopped a few feet away. "Is that dog going to bite me?"

"I don't think so." I put a hand on her to calm her. "She's usually friendly." But today, she'd taken a dislike to two people. I hoped she wasn't ill.

Still casting Caper the occasional cautious look, he turned to Mags. "I didn't know you were here."

"Likewise." Mags crossed her arms. "I thought you left the state years ago."

"I did, but there's no better place to vacation than right here." His grin widened. "How have you been? The house holding up?"

"I live across the lake now. Sold that tinderbox you built when my husband died."

His eyes flashed. "I build good houses."

"So you say, but I heard your company went belly-up. Excuse us, but we're busy. Drive on, CJ."

Frank stepped back, waving off my apology. "She's always been a crusty old woman. Time doesn't seem to have changed that."

Once we were out of earshot, I said, "That wasn't nice. In fact, you were quite rude. You're the one who wanted to stop."

"Took me a minute to figure out his name." She sat in thought for a moment. "We need to make a list of people who need a lot of money. Frank does in order to save his business. You need to research all the other campers."

"That's an invasion of privacy." I shook my head. "Besides, I don't have that kind of time."

"I do."

"I'm not getting you a list of names, Mags." Sometimes my friend was overzealous.

"Fine. I'll figure it out on my own."

I cut her a sideways glance. "How? Do you plan on going up to each site and introducing yourself?"

Her face brightened. "That's a great idea. Thank you."

I groaned and drove back to our side of the lake while eating the sandwich Mags handed me. My spirits lifted at the sight of Eric waiting on my small porch. I quickly dropped Mags off at her house, then drove home to fill my man in on the day's events.

"Hey, gorgeous." His smile always sent my heart flipping. "I see you've got Caper."

I stepped into his open arms. "Danny fetched her for me." I gazed up into his face. "How was your day?"

He gave me a quick kiss and sighed. "Not good. I've got a poacher somewhere. They killed a deer with a bow, then left most of the carcass behind."

"Caper had another leather pouch in the canoe." I took his hand and led him into the house, making sure my dog followed.

His brow furrowed. "Do you know who owns the canoe?"

"I think it's one of the ones for public use. Are you hungry?"

"No, I ate a sandwich. Come sit with me. I've missed you."

It had only been a day, but who was I to deny him? I sat next to him on the loveseat and snuggled close. I told him of making the lead line for Caper, driving around the campground, and Mags's dislike of Frank Dickson.

"I know of him. He's under investigation for insurance fraud, I think. Seems his house burned down under suspicious circumstances."

"Really?" I straightened and stared at him. "That makes him our number-one suspect." Uh oh. I hadn't meant to say anything.

Eric made a noise deep in his throat and covered his eyes with his arm. "Here we go again."

"Someone tried to hurt my dog," I said in defense. "I didn't ask to get involved."

"You don't have to, either." He faced me, his eyes troubled. "I almost lost you once; I don't want to go through that again."

Neither did I, truth be told. Why did trouble seem to follow me?

Chapter Four

Mags bustled up to the outdoor table while I was enjoying my morning coffee. "I have news."

"About?"

She rolled her eyes. "Don't be dense. I spent hours going tent to camper yesterday."

"Okay, what's the news?" I set my coffee down.

"The news is that I don't have any." She plopped down across from me. "Except—" She paused for emphasis and grinned. "Just kidding. Frank Dickson just got out of jail for fraud, and one of those three women who are camping together makes leather crafts. I suspected as much when I saw the headband in Myrna Flutter's hair."

"You shouldn't trespass." Eric hadn't said anything about Dickson spending time behind bars. "How do you know one of the women is into leather?"

"Because I snooped in their tent while they were canoeing on the lake and found the tools used to cut, tan, stretch…you name it."

"I'm sure lots of people enjoy that type of craft, but it does put them on our suspect list."

She beamed. "I'm a regular Sherlock Holmes. Now to see whether any of our residents here can go on that list. I'm going to visit the Flower family. That oldest girl, Rose, got busted for shoplifting last week."

"Really? I hadn't heard." I would have thought she learned her lesson after being suspected of committing the past thefts. "I doubt a just-turned fourteen-year-old could rob a jewelry store, though."

Mags shrugged. "Doesn't hurt to ask. I'll have to do it when her watchdog of a mother isn't around. She doesn't like either of us much."

I didn't blame Lucy. I wouldn't like someone who repeatedly accused a child of mine, either. While Danny had cleaned up his act, Rose still had a way to go. If her mother was a renter, I'd have to consider giving them the boot. As it was, I'd keep a close watch on the girl.

"I'll be making my rounds today checking on the new rentals. Try not to upset too many people, okay?"

"Folks shouldn't be so sensitive. You'd think they'd want to see justice done." She frowned. "Why don't I go with you on your rounds? We can kill two chickens with one axe that way."

I shrugged. "I guess people are used to seeing us together anyway."

"Gee, don't sound so excited." She glanced to where Caper watched us from the end of her leash.

"Poor thing."

"Don't feel sorry for her. I can't have her running off. Besides, I'll take her with us." I drained the last of my coffee, left the cup on the table to retrieve later, and then unhooked Caper. "Come on, sweetie."

I drove to the farthest house, which happened to be the Olsons' two-story home, and turned around to stop at the house before theirs. I didn't know why I always started at the end and worked my way forward, but it made sense to me. Since the houses were placed in numerical order down one side of the curving asphalt road and up the other side, the first place to stop was number fourteen.

An older woman in her mid-sixties, Doris Schultz, had moved in three days ago and said she planned to stay until the Good Lord took her home. After the death of her husband, any other home was too big.

With Caper staying in the cart and Mags on my heels, I climbed the four steps to the front door and knocked. After a few minutes, it cracked open and a brown eye peered out. "Mrs. Schultz, is there anything you need?"

"Peace. There's a dog running around, sniffing in my flower beds."

"I'm sure that won't be a problem anymore." Silly Caper and her enjoyment of digging. I did my best to try and see around the woman, but she wouldn't budge. "Please let me know if you do need anything."

"I'm sure I won't." She slammed the door.

"She's a hoarder," Mags said. "Too embarrassed

to let you inside."

"What makes you say that?"

"Look at the windows. Piled high with boxes, if the crumpled curtains are any indication." She moved the branches of a bush and nodded. "You should see all the junk under here."

This wasn't good. Hopefully, things wouldn't get too far out of control and spill out into the yard. We had a certain standard at Heavenly Acres.

"Under her house would be the perfect place to hide a pouch of diamonds." Mags straightened. "And she did say a dog had been sniffing around."

"Caper isn't the only dog on the property." Although that's where my thoughts had gone, too. "Let's not jump to conclusions."

The renter at number twenty, a college-aged woman named Taylor Bean, opened her door wide to reveal everything done up in pink. I sighed. We'd have to do some painting when she moved out. It wouldn't do any good now to tell her we didn't allow the renters to paint the walls, much less everything. "Good morning," she sang.

"We're making the rounds, checking to make sure you're all settled in for the summer."

"Oh, I am. I love this little house so much I might stay here during my college courses. Most of them are taken online anyway. Thank you for having such great Wi-Fi service."

"Uh, you have to supply your own." I glanced at Mags with wide eyes.

"Oh." Taylor's smile faded. "That's an expense I can't afford. Am I stealing someone's service? Do you think they'll mind? It's Lincoln123. I thought it was named after the president."

"That would be Mr. Lincoln in number three. I suggest you ask him." I smiled and stepped back as she darted down the road.

"That girl is too nice." Mags shook her head. "She's hiding something."

"You've wanted to put every single person we've spoken to on the suspect list. Being nice is not a crime."

"So? Put them all down and do the process of elimination. Isn't that how they do things on those crime shows you watch?"

"They usually have a good reason for putting the person on the list, Mags. Otherwise, you're just wasting time."

"It appears as if we have our own way of doing things." She climbed into the cart. "Onward, driver."

"I feel like I'm driving Miss Daisy."

"Great movie."

By the time we reached house number twenty-five where two young men stayed, my ears ached from Mags's constant speculating. The last thing I wanted to do was visit the other side of the road and then head across the lake. Instead of stopping, I tossed the two vacationers a wave. They looked happy with a beer in their hand. I convinced myself they'd let me know if anything needed fixing.

"Aren't we going to stop?" Mags shot me a dark look. "It's too early in the day to be drinking."

"Which makes them guilty, I presume. They're on vacation. Let them be." I pressed the gas and sped to the campground.

"You're going too fast." Mags slapped my arm. "Why aren't you stopping?"

"I'm barely moving. This speed lets someone flag me down that needs me. I'm tired, and I want to go home."

"At least stop at the leather lady's tent."

I sighed. "Fine." I stopped at site 101 and smiled. Two of the women smiled back. Ioda, the jogger did not. Myrna bent over a set of tools and etched flowers into a leather headband. "Do you make keychains?"

She nodded at my question. "Sure do. Let me fetch them." She ducked into the tent and emerged with five three-inch strips with intricate flower designs.

"How much?"

"Seven dollars."

I chose the one I wanted and fished some money from my pocket. "You do good work."

"I wish it paid more, but thanks."

Mags bumped my shoulder and whispered, "Guilty."

I shot her a dirty look. "Hush."

"Fine. I'll ask." She turned to Myrna. "Do you make leather pouches? The kind someone might put jewels in?"

The woman's eyes widened. "I do. I have a couple missing. Did you find them?"

"Missing?" I asked.

"Someone has been in our tent." Ioda glared. "I always put a piece of tape on the zipper when the three of us leave. Several times the tape has been disturbed. The first day here, Myrna lost some pouches."

That would be the day before the jewel heist. "I'm sorry to hear that, and we will definitely keep an eye out for the missing pouches." I sped away before Mags could say anything more.

"She's lying." Mags glanced back.

"You don't know that. You got into their tent. Someone else could have, too."

"I'll be looking for tape and string the next time I go snooping."

"You'll stay out of people's personal space." I slowed at site 105, saw nothing amiss, and continued to 107. Frank Dickson roasted a hotdog over an open fire, barely registering our presence until Mags called him a jailbird. He scowled and faced us, eating the dog right from the stick.

"Mind your own business, you old hag."

"Well of all the—" Mags's voice rose. "You can't talk to me like—" Her voice faded as I moved away. "CJ."

"It doesn't do any good for you two to get into a name-calling match. We're trying to find a jewel thief, not rehash old feuds."

"I'm capable of doing both. Look. Danny isn't working. He's flirting."

"I haven't given him any jobs today." I stopped the cart and faced her. "What is with you today? You're grumpier than usual."

She sighed and pressed her lips together before speaking. "I found out I have to have a knee replaced. We need to find the thief before I'm out of commission."

I put a hand on her arm. "I'm sorry to hear that.

We'll do what we can, then step back and let the police do the rest while you're recuperating. When's the surgery?"

"Day after tomorrow."

I laughed. "Mags, it's going to be impossible."

"Then I guess I'll be hobbling around on crutches. I don't want you out and about without me. I had to talk you into it, so it's only right I help you."

Caper barked, leaped into Mags's lap, then jumped from the cart and raced away ignoring my demands for her to come back.

"That dog needs obedience school."

I tried to see who she'd gone after, but she zigzagged her way between campsites and disappeared. "We'd best go get her before someone complains." I pressed the gas pedal and zipped along the road, following the sounds of her barking.

"I don't see her," Mags said.

"Neither do I." The barking faded, telling me that Caper was still on the run and getting further ahead of us.

My heart stopped when her bark ended with a yelp.

Chapter Five

We drove around the campground two more times calling her name, but no Caper. My throat burned with unshed tears. My heart feared the worst. Something had happened to my fur child. I leaned my head on the steering wheel and closed my eyes.

"Call Eric." Mags patted my back. "Ask him to come help."

"He's out of range."

"Try anyway."

I straightened and unclipped the radio from my belt and pressed the button. "Come in, Eric." All I received was static. "I told you."

"When is he supposed to be back?"

"Around supper."

"Well, there you go. He'll be home any minute. It's quite possible Caper will beat him home. You know how she likes to wander."

"What about her yelp?" I blinked rapidly to

keep the tears from falling.

"She's also a scaredy-cat. Something spooked her and she's hiding."

I hoped so. I made one more loop around the sites before heading home. Not wanting to miss a sight of the pup, I stayed outside on my tiny porch until time for bed. I'd not seen Caper or Eric and fell asleep with a heavy heart.

When I woke up, I jumped from bed and thundered down the stairs, hoping, praying to see Caper waiting on the porch. Instead, a grinning Eric stood there, a bag of bagels in hand.

"Eager to see me?" His mouth quirked.

"Where were you last night? Caper is missing."

His smile faded. "What do you mean missing?"

I explained about her running off, the yelp, then nothing. "I tried to call, but you didn't answer."

"I just got out of the woods this morning. Almost caught the poacher, too, but he's a sly one." He set the bag on the table and stepped up to take me in his arms. "I'm sorry, sweetheart. We'll find her." He gently lowered me onto the porch chair. "Sit here while I make us coffee."

As if coffee were a cure-all. I just wanted my pain-in-the-butt pet back. I might live in a tiny house, but it seemed too large and empty without her. What if someone hurt her? She was cute and small. Maybe they stole her, and she'd get away and come home. I held onto that hope like a pit bull with a bone. If they left their door open, she'd come home right away. Unless they took her too far for her to find her way back.

I buried my face in my hands. The thief took

her. I knew it deep inside me. She'd been kidnapped to shut her up. All sorts of unsavory thoughts whirled in my head.

"Come to the table." Eric tossed me a sympathetic glance on his way to the picnic table in front of my home. He set the two mugs down and opened the bag. "We'll come up with a plan to find her while we eat."

"She's gone." I slumped on the bench opposite him.

"Maybe not. If the thief took her, as you believe, then they are most likely still here, hiding in plain sight. Just like last time." He spread cream cheese across a multi-grain bagel and handed it to me along with a napkin. "All the diamonds haven't been discovered. The thief won't leave without them."

I looked at him as if he were short a nut or two. "They could have taken the rest of them and left."

He shrugged one shoulder. "Just trying to give you hope."

"Don't give me false hope."

He pierced me with those dark eyes. "I'm sorry. I shouldn't treat you as if you'll break. You're one of the strongest people I know. But listen to me, Clarice Josephine. We will find Caper. I promise."

I wanted to tell him not to make promises he couldn't keep. Instead, I bit into my bagel and stared across the lake. I chose to be optimistic and believe Caper was over there. I needed to search every single tent.

"What's going through that pretty head of yours?"

"A plan."

"Do you mind sharing?"

"You'll tell me not to do it." I kept my gaze on the lake. If I looked at his face, I'd cave.

Eric moved to sit next to me. "I'll come with you."

"You have a poacher to catch."

"What if the poacher is one of the campers?"

I cut him a sideways glance. "Do you really think that?"

"No." He sighed. "I do think they're camping, but not at the campground. So far, we've found remnants of a turkey, a deer, and a razorback. These people are relentless."

"What are they doing with all that meat?"

His lips quirked. "Stockpiling, selling, killing for the sport…who knows?"

"You don't have time to babysit me. You have an important job to do. I'll be fine and stay in the open. I'll take Mags with me. She might get another chance to use her Taser." I chuckled.

Eric shuddered, no doubt remembering the time he'd startled Mags and gotten the shock of his life. "I feel for anyone who walks up behind her." He turned my face fully to his and kissed me. "Promise you'll be careful."

I nodded. "You do the same."

He leaned his forehead against mine. "You know how you feel about Caper missing? Multiply that by one hundred to describe how I'd feel if you were gone."

Sighing, I cupped his cheek. "Thank you."

He kissed me again and stood. "I promise I'll be back to eat supper with you."

"If you're closing in on the poacher, I give you permission to stand me up." I stood and watched as he climbed onto his four-wheeler and roared away. Then I cleaned up our mess and went to get Mags.

"Yippee." She clapped her hands at the news of what we'd be doing that day. The woman got way too excited about snooping. "Let me get my crime bag. I put one together last night."

"Crime bag?"

"Yep. I made you one, but yours is smaller because you're such a sissy." She entered her house, returning a few minutes later with two canvas bags. Hers was a pumpkin orange, mine a sky blue.

I peered inside to see a granola bar, a bottle of water, a notepad and pen, and a bright pink canister of pepper spray. "Looks like we're ready to be gone a while."

"My bag also contains our lunch—ham and cheese sandwiches—and my Taser." Mags climbed into the golf cart. "With the burden you're already carrying about Caper, I didn't want to pile more weight on you."

Silly, sweet woman. There was a huge difference between mental and physical weight, but I appreciated her concern.

As I made our way around the lake, I kept my eyes peeled for any sign of my pup and my ears open for her bark. While I heard the barks and yips of other dogs, I didn't hear her distinctive yelp. My optimism, what little I had, began to fade.

I parked the cart in front of Robinson's trailer. "We walk from here. I want to visit every site. If the people are gone, we'll circle back until we catch them."

"Good thing I wore my walking shoes." Mags lifted one gym shoe-covered foot.

Hitching my so-called crime bag over my shoulder, I headed off with Mags bustling beside me. I hadn't come up with an approach, but figured it a good idea to ask if the campers had registered their pets when they checked in. I'd talk good and loud, so Caper could hear me if she was anywhere around.

After an hour, we'd seen everything from German shepherds to Chihuahuas, but no spaniel mix. I dug my bottle of water out of my bag and took a big gulp as we neared site 101. Lying next to a sack of garbage was Caper's pink rhinestone-covered collar.

I capped the water, glanced at Mags, then marched toward the three women, picking up the collar on my way. "Have you seen the dog this belongs to?"

Carol smiled. "Of course. She wandered into camp yesterday. Myrna found her. In fact, she's in the tent with Myrna as we speak."

"She's my dog." I spit out the words and barged inside the large tent.

Caper, wearing a new leather collar and a muzzle over her square face, jumped up from the bed and ran toward me. A leash brought her up short. My poor baby. I shot a glare at Myrna who worked on yet another headband. "You stole my dog."

The woman's forehead wrinkled. "No, I didn't. She ran in here. I thought she was lost, so I took her in. I planned on posting a note on the bulletin board later today."

"Why the muzzle?" I removed the offending object and cuddled the squirming dog close.

"She's a strange dog. We didn't know yet whether she would bite." Myrna stood and planted her fists on her hips. "I did not steal your dog and resent the implication. You should leave."

"Gladly, and I'm taking my dog with me." I stepped from the tent, almost bumping into Mags who stood guard outside.

She did the two-finger thing from her eyes to each of the other two women. "We're watching y'all."

Ioda rolled hers. "As if an old woman could do anything against three other old women."

Mags made a disgusted sound deep in her throat and stormed to the cart. Head high, shoulders back, she waited for me. "Give me the dog. I promise to hold tight to her while you drive. And I'll remove that ugly collar." She switched the collars and dropped the leather one into my bag.

"Why do you think they switched the collars if they didn't plan on keeping her?" I asked, driving back to my house.

"They lied. No other explanation. They saw this little cutie running loose and snatched her up. You should press charges."

"I can't. It's my fault she wasn't on a leash." I wouldn't make that mistake again. "If the park ranger was anyone but Eric, I'd probably get fined."

"Now that we have the dog back, we can focus on the diamonds."

"We're drawing a blank there, Mags." I took Caper and slid from the cart, then hooked her to her line. "Without more to go on, I don't know where to begin."

"Let's go visit Amber. Maybe Davis let slip something about the investigation."

"Would you call her and invite her over? I don't want to leave Caper so soon." In fact, I didn't intend to leave her alone or off a leash ever again.

Mags made the call. "She'll be right over. Said she was bored and would enjoy the company."

The first words out of Amber's mouth when she joined us at the picnic table were, "Don't ask me about the diamonds."

"Well, why else do you think I called?" Mags pouted.

"To spend time with your granddaughter?" Amber shook her head and sat down. "What have you two been up to?"

I explained about Caper going missing. "I think it's related to the stolen diamonds, but I can't piece together how. Have they located all of them?"

"I can't talk about it, CJ." Amber folded her hands and placed them on the table. "Bill would be so upset."

"Is that Davis's first name? I didn't know." I smiled. "And he won't know if you answer a few simple questions. I need to find out why Caper was put in a canoe and why she was taken yesterday. I suspect it was because she's such a little snoop, but if there are more diamonds out there somewhere, she might be able to find them."

Amber pondered for a minute. "It wasn't only

loose diamonds stolen, but rings, necklaces, etc. Bill believes the jewelry is being taken apart so the diamonds can be sold separately. So to answer your question, there's still a lot not accounted for."

"Good job, sweetie." Mags patted her arm. "You didn't tell us anything confidential."

"You still can't go telling people."

"Mum's the word." Mags pretended to lock her lips.

All I had to do was figure out how to get Caper to find the rest of the loot without going missing again. If I was really unlucky, the thief might come after me.

Chapter Six

The next morning, I pored over the list of names Mags had written on the pad attached to the clipboard and started crossing some off, narrowing the long list down to a few. I might be adding and subtracting as my search went on, but the previous list was too daunting to consider.

I ended up with the three women from site 101 at the top, then Frank Dickson, and Mike and Kim Rowe from house number 10. I still wanted to know why someone here for only a few weeks had so many boxes. I chewed through the end of my pen. With nothing much to go on, these names were just that, names. No apparent motive for any of them. Diamonds? The chance to be rich was a motive. But kidnapping a yappy dog? I didn't get it.

Did Caper really run through site 101 or did they lure her there? Was she chasing someone? The way she'd leaped from the cart led me to believe she was.

"Stop frowning." Mags sat across from me. "You're causing wrinkles. Did Eric make it home alright?"

I nodded. "Not by supper, but he got in around ten and crashed on my sofa, poor guy. He's so tall his legs hang off. I came out here so I wouldn't wake him."

"The case is taking a toll, isn't it?"

"Yes. He's lost weight and looks tired all the time."

She peered at the pad in front of me. "Why'd you cross off all those names?"

"I need a starting point. There were too many."

"Start at the top and work your way down. Everyone knows that. Give me half. I'll do the same thing I did across the water."

"Knock on doors and irritate people?" I held the pad out of her reach. "We'll do this my way, thank you."

"Which means sitting around and waiting for something to happen." She crossed her arms.

"Yes." I glanced past her to see Mrs. Schultz pushing a shopping cart piled high with stuff toward her rental. "Like that. I need to get a look at how bad the inside of her house is."

"I don't see how that's going to help, but I'm curious too." Mags followed me after the woman.

"Hold up, Mrs. Schultz." I stepped between her and the front door. "As overseer here, I need to take a look inside the property."

"Why?" She narrowed her eyes.

"Looking at all the things in that cart and under the house, I need to make sure the interior is safe."

"Of course, it is." She tried to move past me, hitting me in the hip with the basket.

"Ow. There is no negotiation. Your contract says I'm allowed inside with prior notice. I've just given it. I do have a key of my own." I turned and unlocked the front door. I could only open it far enough to squeeze through.

The smell slapped me in the face like a bag of rotten meat. I gagged and pulled the neckline of my tee-shirt over my nose and mouth. How could this have gotten so bad in just a few days? Did the woman actually bring it all with her? Possibly. She'd asked me to leave the key under the mat and arrived during the night while I slept, meeting me outside the next morning. That wouldn't happen again.

A path big enough for a small person to pass through from the front door to the bathroom stretched before me. The house was only four hundred-square feet, but Mrs. Schultz had filled every inch. A glance upward showed a loft filled to the ceiling. Where did she sleep or eat?

I followed the path through garbage, clothes, and boxes until I found a small clearing at the far back in which lay a sleeping bag and a flashlight. At the foot of her "bed" sat a small television. Oh, Mrs. Schultz. I didn't think I'd ever seen anything so sad.

"Satisfied?" I turned to see Mrs. Schultz glaring at me through the open front door.

"This all has to be cleared out, ma'am. The authorities will do it if you don't. I'll be glad to help." God help me with the smell if I had to. I stepped toward the front door. Something rolled under my shoe. I glanced down to see a single sparkling diamond. Using a piece of napkin from the top of the nearest pile, I picked it up. "Where did you get this?"

"By the water. It was lying there in the mud. Pretty, isn't it?"

I squeezed past her and into the fresh air and took a big gulp of air. Since I knew little to nothing about gems, I didn't know whether it was real or cubic zirconia. But Davis might. "Are you aware of the jewel heist a few days ago?"

"Of course. I don't live in a cave," she sneered.

"I need to take this."

"Oh, no, you don't. That is mine. Finders keepers." She reached for the jewel.

Mags slapped her hand. "This is police business. If it isn't stolen, you'll get it back."

"You assaulted me."

"I'm going to do a lot worse if you don't settle down."

"Ladies, please." The situation was quickly spiraling out of control. Seeing Eric approach us was like a drink of ice water after wandering in the desert for several days.

"Good morning." He smiled down at me. "Why didn't you wake me? I'm late for work."

"You needed the rest." I opened my hand. "Mrs. Schultz found this. Can you tell if it's real?"

"No. I'd take it to Davis, but I've got to run." He gave me a quick kiss. "I think I'll catch the poacher today. I'm running out of places for them to hide."

"Good luck." I watched him jog away before I

pulled my cell phone from my belt and called Davis. He promised to be there in a few minutes, which, since he was at Amber's, was less than five.

I handed him the diamond. "Is it part of the stolen loot?"

He shrugged. "I'll have to get it tested." He dropped it into the front pocket of his dress shirt.

Mrs. Schultz gasped. "That's mine."

He glanced over, his eyes widening at the sight of what lay beyond the open front door. "Ma'am, you've got to clean that up before I call the health inspector. As for the gem, if it isn't stolen, you'll get it back pronto." He shook his head and strode to the sedan parked in front of house number four.

"Now will you put her name back on the list?" Mags raised an eyebrow.

"Until we hear from Davis, yes." My gaze followed Rose slipping in and out between the houses. When she reached number ten, she stopped and peeked in the window.

Mike Rowe stormed out the front door and shook her. "How many times have I told you to stop spying on us?"

I sprinted forward to stop him from hurting the girl. "Mr. Rowe?"

His hands slipped from Rose's shoulder. "I've warned her, Miss Turley."

"Rose?" I tilted my head. "It's wrong to peek in people's windows."

"They're doing some weird stuff in there. I want to make sure it isn't a meth lab that will blow us all up." She crossed her arms and gave the sullen look only a teenage girl could.

I turned to the man. "Sir?"

He huffed. "I work from home. My wife and I design fragrances for perfumes and soaps."

"Mind if I take a look inside?"

"Go ahead." He waved an arm and gave an insolent bow.

I stepped into the best smelling house ever. Florals, spices, and pine wafted over me. Mrs. Rowe bent over a line of glass tubes. The mystery of what all the boxes contained had been solved. "Why here?" I asked.

"We work from home," she said, glancing up, "but we're still on vacation. Where we go, our supplies go in case inspiration hits."

"Must cost a lot." Mags snuck up behind me.

Mrs. Rowe blinked rapidly. "I guess, but we obviously make enough to pay our expenses or we wouldn't be doing this."

"Off the suspect list," Mags muttered.

"Never mind her," I said. "She's having knee surgery tomorrow and isn't herself." I took my friend by the arm and escorted her from the house. "Not off the list," I whispered. "The tennis bracelet on her wrist is worth a fortune if it's real."

"Ooh." Her eyes bugged. "Promise no sleuthing until I'm up and around. I figure the next day I'll be good to go."

I laughed. "That would be a miracle, my friend."

"Take care of my flowers."

"Either I will or I'll have Tammy do it."

"Nope. She's still working on typing up all those family letters of mine." Mags gave me a finger wave and veered off as we reached her house.

I collected Caper and took her for a walk. The dog strained against her leash to investigate each house we passed. If it were only one or two, I'd think she might actually have bloodhound in her. As it was, my dog was just nosy.

We strolled along the water's edge, stopping near the log Eric and I sat on, sometimes talking, sometimes not. As I watched the sun sparkle on the mirror surface of the water, Rose skipped rocks a short distance away. I groaned but called her over anyway.

"What?"

"Do you always expect someone to have something bad to say?"

She shrugged, tossing back her dark hair. "Seems like that's the way it is."

Unfortunately, it was the case now. "I need you to stop getting into trouble. I know your mother has little options in being able to afford a roof over the heads of all you children, but if I get too many complaints—"

"You'd kick a widow and her kids to the street?" She paled.

"Not me, but the owner might. Surely you know what you're doing is wrong? Out past curfew, peeking in windows. Does your mother think this behavior is okay?"

Rose shrugged again. "She's too busy to pay much attention to me."

Poor thing. I needed to find a way to keep her out of trouble, and there wasn't a lot of money left in the monthly budget to give her a job. "What kinds of things do you like to do?"

"I don't know."

"Do you like flowers? The common area could use some love."

"Are you serious? My last name is Flower. My first is Rose. Do you think I might be tired of flowers? Yuck." She stormed away, leaving me feeling as if I'd been chastised.

I'd still think of something for her to do, but it would take a little time. Maybe she could help Mags after her surgery. I chuckled thinking of my outspoken friend and the surly teen spending hours together. I'd speak to Mags first chance I got.

Caper dug around the log I sat on, sniffling like a little pig. I tugged on the leash; she resisted.

"What is so interesting under there?" I got on my knees and peered into the log. "I'm not sticking my hand where things decay and bugs roam, little girl. You can just forget all about that." Until I saw something sparkle from inside a mesh bag.

Then, something hit me in the back of the head, and the world went dark.

Chapter Seven

"CJ?" Something shook me and licked my face. Wait. Not the same person.

I opened my eyes and gazed into the worried face of Eric while Caper jumped on my chest and licked my face. "Off." Oh, my head ached.

"Are you alright?" Eric helped me to a sitting position. "What happened?"

"I found something shiny inside this log. The next thing I knew, someone hit me from behind." I felt the knot on the back of my head, relieved to discover I wasn't bleeding. My eyes widened. "More diamonds. Only this time they were in a mesh bag."

Eric shined his flashlight in the log. "Nothing there now. Let's get you home and call Davis."

With his arm around my waist, he helped me up. Caper yipped and bounded around our feet. Since bending over made me nauseous, I'd have to let her leash trail behind her.

Eric settled me on the sofa, closed the door to keep my dog inside, and dialed Davis. He explained the situation, then hung up. "He's sending Milton and Lowery. I also called Amber to come take a look at your head."

"Why can't Davis come?"

"He said he was busy." Eric sat beside me and took my right hand in his. "Can I get you anything?"

I shook my head. "All I was doing was sitting. Why would the thief hide the diamonds all over the place? Why not put the whole lot in one safe spot?"

"In case some of them were found, maybe. That way they wouldn't lose them all." He leaned against the back of the sofa. "Or in case they went to jail, they could come back after they were released and get them. Who knows? All I do know is they're smart enough not to sell them all at once and attract attention."

"Has any showed up anywhere?"

He shook his head. "My guess is they're finding private buyers."

"Which makes it harder for us." For the last rash of robberies, the culprit had tried selling the items online. I didn't think that would happen with the gems.

We sat silently, eyes closed until a knock sounded on the door. Eric put his hand on my knee. "I'll get it."

Amber, dressed in her scrubs, rushed into the house. "Is this going to be a common occurrence, CJ?"

"Unfortunately." I sat still occasionally wincing

while she poked and prodded.

"Just a bad knot. Maybe a slight concussion. You'll have a doozy of a headache."

"I already do." I accepted the aspirin she handed me. "Thanks for coming."

"Milton and the rookie were pulling up as I did. I wonder why—"

In answer to her question, another knock sounded, this one louder and longer. Jerk.

Milton entered, a stupid grin on his square face. "People are still trying to knock some sense into you, huh?"

Lowery rolled her eyes. "You were attacked?"

I nodded and repeated everything I'd told Eric. "I didn't see them, hear them, or smell them. I can't say whether it was a man or a woman."

"Not much to go on," Lowery said. "I'll go take a look at the area. Maybe they left some prints."

Doubtful since the log sat in thick grass, but it wouldn't hurt. Since the tiny house was filled to capacity, Amber excused herself, promising to come by in the morning before work to check on me.

Milton simply stared without blinking for several minutes. "You're getting involved again, aren't you? What? A glutton for punishment?"

"I've already told her all that." Eric resumed his seat next to me. "In CJ's defense, she hasn't actively looked for the diamonds. Only her missing dog has, right?" He glanced at me.

"Right. Caper has a talent for finding shiny things, then she disappeared yesterday. I was just sitting and watching the sunset over the water when

I was assaulted." Now, things had become personal. I might not have been actively investigating before, but I would be now. Somewhere there were more diamonds that the thief thought I either had or knew where they were.

"I recognize that stubborn look." Eric leaned his head back and focused on the ceiling.

Lowery returned. "Not a thing, other than disturbed debris inside the log. Are there any empty campsites? Maybe I should go undercover."

"That's pretty optimistic for a rookie," Milton said, glowering.

"I'm new enough people don't know who I am yet. It could work. I'm a trained law-enforcement officer. I might see what civilians miss."

Personally, I thought it an excellent idea. With Eric involved in work problems of his own, having a cop around could be a very good thing. "I like it."

"You don't have a say," Milton said.

"Hurry up and figure it out. I need to go to bed so I can help Mags after her surgery tomorrow. Amber is bringing her home, then I'll make sure she's settled. I need my sleep."

That's all it took to clear out my house. Eric stood at the bottom of the stairs to make sure I made it up without falling, blew me a kiss, then locked the door and pulled it closed.

My head still ached when I woke the next morning, but only when I touched the spot where I'd been hit. I downed a protein shake for breakfast, then made the rounds until I received a text from Amber saying they were on their way home. That was my cue to go to number six and talk to Lucy and Rose Flower.

Lucy listened to my proposal without speaking, then turned to Rose. "It's a good idea. You need to learn to think of someone other than yourself. Taking care of Mags while she recovers is perfect."

"My whole summer is ruined." Rose threw her head back and groaned.

"You should have thought about that before getting into trouble." A crash from inside the house sent Lucy rushing away from us. "Take her with you now," she tossed over her shoulder.

"You heard your mom." I patted the seat beside me. "There's no time like the present to get started."

Making whining noises, Rose climbed into the cart. "I don't like you."

"Sorry about that, but you won't like everyone in life. Don't give me a hard time. I have a headache." I turned us around and stopped in front of Mags's place, relieved to see Amber's car parked out front. "Good. They're here."

With Rose lagging behind, I knocked, then entered Mags's house. "Sit there." I pointed to the sofa before making my way to the small bedroom at one end of the house. "Hey, Mags. How are you feeling?"

She glanced up with bleary eyes. "Fine right now. Pain medication is a blast. Reminds me of the sixties."

"Grandma, you were a kid in the sixties?" Amber shook her head.

"I read. I watch television."

"I've brought someone to help you until you're up and around," I said. I motioned my hand for

Rose to join us.

Mags frowned. "Nope."

"You'll be helping her out. She's bored and needs something to do."

"I'm not crazy about it either, lady." Rose crossed her arms.

"Then go away."

"Mags," I warned. "You'll need help and the rest of us are busy. Rose is the perfect solution. It's only temporary."

She glanced over at Amber who nodded. Mags's brows lowered. "Traitors, both of you."

Amber placed a tender kiss on her grandmother's cheek. "I'll be back later to check on you." She transferred her attention to me. "How are you doing?"

"Fine. The spot is tender, but that's it."

"What happened to you?" Mags winced and scooted to a better sitting position.

I explained for the third time in less than twenty-four hours what had happened to me. "I'm fine, though. No worries."

"I saw someone out last night," Rose spoke up. "They were walking real slow around the lake as if they were looking for something. I didn't see them hit you because my mom called me home, but they were headed in that direction."

All three of us turned to stare.

"What did they look like?" I asked.

She hitched her chin. "I'm not saying another thing unless Mags agrees to be nice to me."

"See what I mean?" Mags's eyebrows rose. "You want me to spend every day with this girl?"

"It won't hurt you to be nice," Amber said.

"It might. Besides, she's nothing more than a child and doesn't need to be privy to a crime investigation." Mags crossed her arms to match Rose.

"For crying out loud. Rose, tell us what you saw. Mags promises to be nice." I sighed. "I feel as if I'm babysitting."

"Fine. I'll be the grownup." Rose took a deep breath. "I'm pretty sure it wasn't a man, because the person wasn't much taller than you, CJ. But they were…kind of fat." She made an apologetic gesture with her hands. "They wore baseball caps, baggie tee-shirts, and jeans, I think. Oh, and scarves, maybe. Something was blowing behind them."

Could fit any number of people. Might be the thief, an accomplice, or just a hired thug paid to fetch the loot. It also didn't confirm the suspect as male. "I'll pass this on to Detective Davis. Thank you."

Amber and I left Mags in bed and Rose playing on her cell phone. "That went as well as expected," Amber said once we were outside.

"At least they haven't killed each other." I grinned. "I'm headed back to the campground to look for anyone that matches the description Rose gave us. Do you want me to text Davis or will you tell him?"

"I'm meeting him for lunch, so I'll pass it on. Be careful, CJ. They've already hit you once."

"Don't have to tell me twice."

"Right." She laughed. "See you later."

I tossed her a wave and climbed into my cart.

After collecting my dog and letting her do her business, I clipped her leash to the cart. "Ready to do some more snooping?"

She panted in response and leaned her paws on the dashboard.

It was a good thing I was filling in for Robinson. Otherwise my many trips around the sites would seem suspicious. As it was, the campers seemed adjusted to the sight of me. Most of them didn't glance my way. Not seeing anyone who looked like the person Rose described, I parked by the bulletin board to wait for Lowery.

She showed up less than an hour later. "Sorry. Both Davis and Milton had to grill me on safety. Why is it men think women less intelligent? I have no intention of stepping in harm's way. I'm here strictly for surveillance."

"We're both on the petite side," I said with a shrug. "Makes them want to be protective, I guess. You're in site 102, right next to the three women on my suspect list. They're also the ones who had my dog." I ruffled Caper's ears.

"Perfect. My story is—" She twisted her lips. "I'm taking a break from an abusive husband, trying to figure out my next step. This way people will feel sorry for me and grow comfortable enough to confide in me, I hope." She grinned. "They might say something incriminating."

"Let's hope so." I followed her to the site, helped her unload and set up her tent, which turned out not to be a skill of mine. Despite my anger at the three women of 101 after they abducted Caper, I smiled and waved and introduced their neighbor.

"How long are you ladies staying?"

Myrna shrugged. "Until you need the site, I guess. No determinate amount of time. None of us have anywhere we need to be. Is that alright?"

"I have enough people coming and going that it shouldn't be a problem." Strange to want to camp for an extended period of time without a camper. Dickson also didn't seem in a hurry to leave. If that were the case, why didn't they all just rent one of the tiny houses before they filled up for the summer?

Things got stranger and stranger.

Chapter Eight

After a restless night thinking of every reason someone might camp in a tent for weeks, I decided to ask. The curiosity wouldn't leave me.

Davis exited his car when I stepped outside with Caper in my arms. "How's the head?"

"Much better, thank you. The knot is going down, but the area is still tender." I smiled. "What's up?"

"The diamond found in Mrs. Schultz's home was a cubic zirconia. If she found it by the lake, it most likely fell out of someone's costume jewelry. Amber also passed on the description of the person Rose saw. Mind if I look at your CTV camera footage?"

"Of course." Dunce. Since I'd had the cameras installed a few months ago, I should have thought of that very thing. But I'd grown so accustomed to them and forgot. "Wait here. I'll bring my laptop outside." I hooked Caper to her lead and retrieved my computer, feeling as if I'd let my tenants down by being irresponsible.

I set the laptop on the table and pulled up the camera footage. The camera caught me being hit by the person Rose described, then the criminal gave Caper a swift kick sending her running into the bushes. I'd give them a kick they wouldn't forget when I found out who the person was. "You can't see the person's face." My shoulders slumped.

"We also can't tell whether it's a man or a woman, but I don't think they're fat." Davis stood. "They purposely wore baggy clothes to hide their body shape. This isn't an amateur."

"Eric and I think this person has hidden the diamonds all over the place in order not to be caught with the lot all at once."

"Good assumption. Be careful, CJ. We don't want a repeat of what happened a few months ago." He pulled the cubic zirconia from his pocket and handed it to me. "Your tenant will be happy to get it back."

"Yes, it's one more thing to add to her clutter."

"The fire inspector is paying her a visit this afternoon. You might want to warn her." He headed back to his car, leaving me with the unpleasant task of reminding Mrs. Schultz to clean her house. It might be more effective if Davis told her.

I unhooked Caper and transferred her and her leash to the golf cart, then headed reluctantly toward number fourteen. I stopped at the sight of Rose sitting on Mags's porch, her chin in her hand. "What's wrong?"

"Mags didn't like the breakfast I made her."

"What did you fix?"

"A bowl of Lucky Charms." She exhaled heavily. "Who doesn't like that?"

"Apparently Mags. Where did you get the cereal?"

"I brought it with me. I don't like to eat that stuff that tastes like cardboard." Her eyes widened. "That's all Mags had."

I smiled. "Maybe tomorrow you can eat what you want and fix her what she wants. She likes ham and cheese sandwiches if you're looking for a lunch idea. Oh, and the person you saw by the lake...that's the person who clobbered me. Thanks for being so observant."

That seemed to cheer her up. "I'll pay even better attention from now on. Maybe I'll have a part in catching the guy." She leaped to her feet and ducked into the house at the sound of a bell ringing.

I hoped the girl didn't get too involved. I wouldn't want to put her in harm's way. Her mother would kill me. So, I did the right thing and yelled after her not to do anything stupid before driving away.

It was obvious before I knocked on Mrs. Schultz's door that she hadn't started cleaning out her house. I knocked again and waited for her to answer.

"I'm busy doing what you told me," she said immediately upon opening the door an inch.

"It doesn't appear that way." I took a deep breath. "The fire inspector is coming later today to take a look. It's safe to say he'll give you a deadline. How do you even know what's in here?"

"I know. It may look like chaos to you, but it's organized chaos."

I handed her the cubic zirconia. "Not real."

"Thank you for bringing it back."

"May I ask you where you find all your…treasures?"

"Here and there. Lately, I've scored at the campground and swimming beach. It's amazing what people leave behind or throw away. Look what I found yesterday, just lying in the grass." She held up a leather pouch like the one the diamonds were in. "I can put all kinds of things in this."

"Was it empty when you found it?"

She nodded. "Unfortunately. I found this in the children's play area." She held up an empty mesh bag.

I needed to let Davis know about the person who hit me and removed the diamonds. "Please be prepared for the inspector. When you're ready to start cleaning, let me know. I'll help you." I heard the door close as I climbed into the cart. I texted Davis about Mrs. Schultz finding the two bags. Let him deal with forcing the evidence away from her.

As I headed for the campgrounds, I spotted Eric driving toward me. I smiled, my heart leaping as usual at the sight of him. "Catch the poacher?"

He grinned. "I did. Two men now behind bars. What are you up to? I'd like to tag along and spend some time with you. I've missed you."

I told him of the person caught on camera. "I'm driving around to see whether anyone matches the description."

He parked the four-wheeler on the side of the

road, scooped Caper into his arms, and took her place on the passenger seat. "All right, Sherlock, proceed."

"I guess that makes you Watson." I laughed, pleased he let me be the famous detective.

We stopped at site 101 where the three women sat, stainless-steel wine glasses in hand, toasting something. I introduced Eric, which garnered the same response as in the past. No matter how old a woman was, she wasn't immune to his good looks and charm.

When they finished tossing out flirtatious remarks, I asked, "Forgive me, ladies, but I just can't figure out why the three of you are staying in a tent long term when you could have rented one of the tiny houses."

Ioda shot a glance at Myrna, then answered, "It's kind of personal."

Myrna frowned. "I lost my house. This is the cheapest alternative. My sweet friends here have agreed to spend some time with me until I'm able to get on my feet."

Nice of them, but why not let her live with one of them? That seemed more like a friend thing than living so primitively.

I wanted to ask what Myrna did for a living, but restrained myself. It didn't seem possible she could make a living off her leather products unless she had an inventory somewhere and sold online. None of my business as long as she paid for the campsite.

"The next site is rented by Frank Dickson, someone Mags used to know. No love lost between the two."

"Why make it a point to stop at these two?" Eric asked.

"They're both long-term campers, which makes no sense to me. Both need money. Diamonds are a lot of money."

"As good a reason as any. I told you about Dickson, remember?"

"Oh, right."

"Anyone else on your suspect list?"

"I did have the couple in house number ten, but all the boxes they brought on vacation with them are related to their fragrance business. I really don't have much to go on except the thief's description, and I'm not seeing anyone today who matches it."

Eric propped his feet on the dashboard. "Despite what you say, I know you like solving these mysteries, but this might be one you can't."

"The stealing of the diamonds and the kidnapping of Caper are linked somehow. It might not be easy, but I'll figure it out." Instead of heading to Dickson's site, I continued the drive around the loop, studying everyone in sight for their characteristic gait.

"The way you're glaring at everyone isn't very subtle," Eric said with a laugh. "One old man looked frightened as we drove by."

"Sorry, I'm just so determined to find out who actually thinks a dog can point them out as a crook." Caper might be smart and a bit rowdy and undisciplined, but she couldn't talk. I pasted on a smile that sent Eric into a fit of laughter.

"Now you look like a shark ready to attack." He snorted.

I gave him a playful slap. "I can't help the way I look."

He kissed the side of my neck. "You're such a pretty shark."

My face heated, despite the big grin on my face. If only we could find the thief as easily as Eric could distract me.

Not finding anyone matching the description of the one I sought, I drove us to Mags's house. "You don't mind, do you? I want to check on her."

"I'm yours for the day. I go where you go. Besides, it'll be good to see her." He straightened back in his seat.

I hadn't parked the cart yet before Rose stormed out of the house yelling, "Suck it up, Buttercup."

I bit back a smile. "What's happening?"

"She's a pain in my rear." Rose crossed her arms and glowered. "I fixed her that stupid cardboard cereal and gave her a pain pill. She wants another one and it hasn't been four hours. Are you paying me to watch her because I deserve to get paid. She's impossible." She plopped down on the top step.

"I'll make sure you get paid." I climbed from the cart and took Caper from Eric's lap. "Watch the dog, and I'll go talk to Mags."

I found my friend propped up in bed, brow creased, lips downturned. "What's going on here?"

"Rose is an evil girl. I'm in pain and want out of this bed. I can't get out unless I have a pain med. Then she insists I'm too unstable on my feet to get up when I'm drugged." Her lips twitched. "She might have something there. That child will make a great nurse someday."

"Then why are you giving her such a hard time?" I perched on the foot of her bed.

"Boredom, plain and simple. Entertain me."

I told her about the video of me getting hit in the head. "Eric and I drove all over this place and didn't see anyone who remotely resembled that person. Maybe they don't live here but want us to think they do."

"What if you're dealing with more than one person?"

"What?" My mouth dropped open.

"Someone had to drive the getaway car, right?" Mags tilted her head. "It would be difficult indeed for one person to pull off a heist like that. I'd definitely say you need to consider more than one person."

"You are a genius." I patted her good leg. "Hurry up and get well enough for crutches. I obviously need your brain power."

"Obviously." She smiled. "You need to keep me updated a few times a day. If I had something to focus on, I wouldn't torment Rose as much. Does Eric have another radio? Then we could have constant communication."

I wasn't sure I could handle twenty-four/seven of Mags, but promised to ask. It was only temporary after all, right?

Chapter Nine

My radio crackled at five a.m. "Yeah?" I held the radio up against my ear. It took a few seconds to realize I needed to hold down the talk button. I tried again. "Yeah?"

"Did you ever see *Rear Window*?" Mags asked.

"The Alfred Hitchcock movie?" I laid my arm across my eyes. "Do you know what time it is?"

"Yes to both questions."

"What do you want?" I wasn't the friendliest person early in the morning.

"I couldn't sleep, so I hobbled to the front window to watch the day start. I saw someone nosing around your house."

That got me sitting up. "Why didn't you lead with that information?" I crawled to the small window in my loft and peeked through a crack in the curtain. "I don't see anyone."

"That's because they aren't there anymore, but I thought you might want to know that someone was there a few minutes ago. I'll let you go back to sleep now. Ciao." Click.

There was no way I could go back to sleep. I should go outside to investigate, but the memories of being taken at gunpoint to the chapel in the woods prevented such idiocy a second time. I called Eric.

"Hello?" His voice sounded as if I woke him.

"I thought you were usually up by now. I'm sorry."

"It's fine. I'm just catching up on my shut-eye. Are you alright?"

I told him of Mags's radio call. "Will you come check outside with me?"

"I'll be there in ten." Click.

That sweet man never kept me waiting for long. Since I wasn't used to such attention, I had to be careful not to take advantage of his kindness. To make up for waking him, I rushed downstairs to make coffee and omelets. By the time he knocked on my door, breakfast was almost finished. I rushed to the door. "Good morning. I made breakfast."

"Good, since you woke me up." He smiled, then kissed me. "I didn't mind. It makes me feel good that you want me to keep you safe. Let's take a quick look outside, then eat."

I nodded and followed him outside. The sun had risen just enough for us to see a set of footprints in the soft dirt around my azalea bushes. I snapped a picture with my cell phone. "I guess Mags wasn't imagining things after all."

"No, and Davis is going to get tired of us calling him. Maybe I should call you Trouble." Still smiling despite the early hour, Eric placed the call before saying we could eat and Davis would get here when he could. "This diamond heist has the department stretched thin."

"Which is why I'm surprised he isn't sending Milton and Lowery."

Eric shrugged. "Too many calls from us, I guess. He muttered something about things getting serious." With his hand on the small of my back, sending ripples of pleasure through me, he guided me into the house.

We ate breakfast at the small fold-down table in the space between what I called my living room and my kitchen. Only big enough for two, any meals eaten inside were cozy, and Eric's knees pressed against mine. After we finished, I made another pot of coffee and set mugs, coffee, and creamer on a tray. We'd meet Davis outside. My house wasn't big enough for two men over six feet tall.

A tired-looking detective joined us as I started my second cup of coffee. He accepted a mug with thanks and sat next to Eric at the picnic table. "I've got nothing."

I texted him the photo I'd taken earlier. "Now you have a footprint. Don't forget a physical description."

"The person might as well be a ghost."

"More than one. Mags said they would have had a driver." It wasn't like him to be so despondent.

He shot me a sharp glance. "She's too smart for her own good."

So, he already suspected as much. Mags is worse now that she's housebound and has a radio.

Boredom threatens to make her a trifle annoying."

"God help us all." Davis shuddered. "I hate to put more on your plate, Eric, but once again, I need you to try and keep CJ and Mags from sticking their noses where they don't belong."

All three of us turned as Rose sprinted past, whipped around, and headed back to Mags's. From the look on the girl's face, I surmised she fled to keep from throttling the old woman. As if an afterthought, she turned around and joined us.

"Mags told me about someone snooping around your house. Can I see the photo of the footprint? I'm kind of an expert on shoes," she said proudly.

"How did you know I took a picture?" I asked.

She looked at me as if I'd said she didn't know me.

I showed her the photo.

"Keds, I'm pretty sure. She flashed a grin and strolled back to her job.

"Hmm." Davis exhaled sharply. "Again, too many people involved messing up my investigation."

"It takes a village," I offered.

"We aren't raising a child." He took another sip of his coffee and returned to his squad car.

"At least I have one more thing to watch for on my rounds," I told Eric. "I can now look at people's feet."

"That won't be obvious at all."

I laughed, knowing that if the wrong person noticed, I'd be flushing out a crook. My laugh cut off as fast as it started. Flushing out a crook would put me in danger again. I peered up at Eric from lowered lashes. The man cared for me, but I also knew he'd only put up with so much before putting a stop to my investigating. I silently vowed I'd quit if things got even close to the level of danger they were a few months ago.

"What are you thinking, CJ?" Eric reached across the table and put his hand over mine. "You're somewhere else."

"Trying to think of how to find this person without dying." Honesty was best, right?

"I like that idea." He pulled back, his dark gaze settling on me with the warmth of a summer sun. "I'm free to be your bodyguard unless something comes up at work."

"You're a much better-looking sidekick than Mags." Knowing how much he enjoyed my company still set me back a bit. I'd spent so many years caring for Grams before her death, I'd never experienced dating or physical attraction. Sometimes it was hard not to act like a giddy schoolgirl because of my inexperience in the romance department of life.

"Thanks." Eric chuckled. "So, ready to go looking at feet?"

"I have to make the rounds anyway." I gathered the coffee mugs and carried them into the house before collecting Caper. Eric already sat in the driver's seat, grinning like a goon because he knew how much I liked driving. "Hey."

"Your driving scares me. You take corners way too fast." He winked.

"Fine." I winked back and climbed in the passenger side. "But I also stop a lot to check things out."

"Oh, I plan on stopping." He motioned his head toward the back of the cart.

I leaned over the seat to see a wicker picnic basket. "Yay."

He tugged me back into my seat, keeping a hold on my hand. "It occurred to me we've never had a 'real' date. I intend to remedy that. The picnic is only the beginning, sweetheart."

My face flushed, as it seemed to do a lot when Eric was around. "I'd like that." I sat back and enjoyed the feel of my hand in his strong one.

Eric wasn't kidding about driving. We went at a turtle's pace around the campsites, waving and stopping to chat as if we didn't have a care in the world. I kept a friendly smile on my face as I glanced at sandaled foot after sandaled foot and hiking boots galore. I didn't see anything resembling a Keds until we stopped at site 105 where the two young men camped. After close inspection, their shoes were Vans and not what I was looking for.

"You guys need to clean up this site," I said, spotting multiple beer cans strewn around. "There's a trash can and a recycling bin twenty steps away."

"We will. We're going on a hike, then packing up to leave tomorrow afternoon," one of them said. "Can it wait?"

"It cannot," Eric added. He turned off the cart, fully prepared for us to sit while they cleaned up.

Muttering and groaning, the two men acted like teenagers asked to clean their rooms. Robinson took pride in the campgrounds, and as his substitute, so did I.

Caper kept a close watch on them, her tail wagging, but didn't try to jump from the cart. Maybe her adventures the last few days made her a little warier of strangers.

When they'd cleaned the site to our satisfaction, Eric asked, "Where you two headed on a hike? Did you inform anyone in case you go missing?"

"We told those ladies in site 101," the dark-haired one said. "They seemed awfully interested in where we were going. You don't think they plan on stealing our beer, do you?"

"If you're worried, you might want to lock your valuables in your car." Eric shot me an amused glance. "Although there might be others more interested in your beer than those ladies."

I agreed. Wine was their choice of drink.

The man shrugged. "We're headed up the waterfall trail. We're up to the ten-mile hike and have water and food in our backpacks."

Eric nodded. "Smart thinking."

I knew he'd be by after dark to see whether the men had returned safely. I intended to be back earlier than that to search their tent. Someone close by was our thief, and I would find out who until the evidence pointed elsewhere. Was it trespassing to look inside tents if I was responsible for the campground?

When we drove off, Eric said, "I know your mind is whirling. What crazy scheme are you cooking up now?"

"I want to search their tent when they leave. Not only theirs, but any other empty tents. The diamonds and a pair of Keds are somewhere."

"I suppose you're going to want me to stand guard."

"Would you?" I kissed his cheek. "Thanks."

He groaned. "If people start complaining, Robinson will never ask you to take over again."

We continued our slow drive until lunchtime. Eric turned off the asphalt and onto a dirt trail. We climbed from the cart and headed to the cleared grassy area in front of the giant cross that lit up at night. With the newly renovated chapel in back of us and the lake in front of us, we'd enjoy our picnic in one of the most beautiful, peaceful places around.

Hard-boiled eggs, bacon, and sharp cheddar cheese made up our simple lunch along with tea flavored with muscadine juice. The meal couldn't be more perfect. After I ate, I leaned back on my hands. "I absolutely love it here. I'm so glad I didn't choose to stay in Grams' house."

"Do you ever plan on selling it?" Eric stretched out next to me, balanced on his elbow and gazed at my face.

"No, it's a nice Victorian over a hundred-years-old. Someday, I might want to move back."

"When you're married with kids?" His eyes twinkled.

"Maybe." I stared back at the water before I said something stupid like, "maybe with you."

"I love the way your face turns pink when our conversation turns personal," Eric said, reaching up and tucking a dandelion behind my ear. "I've never met anyone as sweet and unjaded as you."

"I've been pretty sheltered my whole life."

"Is that why you jump into a mystery with both feet? Not enough adventure when you were younger?"

I shrugged. "Probably. That and growing up on Nancy Drew." I smiled.

A scream shattered the afternoon, sending us both to our feet.

A woman struggled in the lake, submerged, then came up sputtering.

Without removing his boots, Eric dove into the water.

With my heart in my throat, I watched as Eric swam with strong strokes toward the drowning woman. She slapped at him and tried to climb on Eric's shoulders until he wrapped his arm around her neck and pulled her toward shore.

I waded knee deep to help, grabbing one of her arms and assisting Eric in laying her on the thick grass. I recognized her from the campground as renting site 102 with her husband. She took in deep ragged breaths. I knelt on the grass beside her and placed a consoling hand on her shoulder while Eric called for an ambulance.

"Someone...pushed...me," she gasped. "My husband is still out there."

Eric dove back into the water.

Chapter Ten

"Are you sure?" I glanced up at Eric.

"Yes." The woman struggled to a sitting position. "I'm into geocaching and was following the coordinates to one when someone pushed me off the pier."

"You didn't see them?"

"No. I heard footsteps, but the pier is a busy place. I can't swim. Neither can my husband." Tears ran down her face. "I'm pretty sure he was pushed over, too."

While Eric swam back toward the dock, I waited next to the woman and called Davis. The ambulance arrived before Milton and Lowery. They placed an oxygen mask over Mrs. Goads' face, and waited until the police gave them the all-clear since her situation wasn't life-threatening.

When the police arrived, Milton raced down the bank toward the pier, supposedly to help Eric find Mr. Goads. Lowery stopped next to me and the woman. She had the woman go over her story again.

"Geocaching?" Lowery's brow wrinkled. "Like a treasure hunt?"

"Sort of. Mike and I like to compete to see who can find the cache first."

"I think there's something there other than a piece of paper to sign and a coin or Happy Meal toy," I said, explaining to the officer that geocaching was indeed like treasure hunting and very popular.

"The coordinates led to the dock?"

Mrs. Goads nodded. "As close as we could figure."

Lowery called Milton on her radio and suggested they tape off the dock to prevent spectators from messing up a potential crime scene. "She's free to go," she told the paramedics.

"I'm not going anywhere until my husband is found." She pushed the oxygen mask away.

The longer it took Eric to find the man, the more my handsome ranger dove beneath the water, and the less the chance of finding Mr. Goads alive. "Can your husband swim?"

"Yes. Very well, in fact." She kept her gaze locked on the dock, then hopped off the gurney and bolted around the lake.

I glanced at a shocked Lowery, then gave chase, the officer right beside me. Our feet pounded the packed soil at the lake's edge.

Lowery stopped at the end of the dock. "You can't go any further, CJ. I'll fetch Mrs. Goads and have her stay here with you while we search." The shadow flickering across her face told us she didn't think they'd find the husband alive.

I agreed. If he had been pushed, hit his head, or gotten ensnared in something under the wooden dock, he'd have been underwater way too long to survive. From the way his wife wrapped her arms around her middle and paced the shore, she was giving up hope of finding him alive.

Sobs wracked her body. Her gaze shifted from the ground to the water to the ground. I went to her and put an arm around her shoulder, leading her to a bench at the lake's edge. It wasn't until Caper climbed into the woman's lap that I realized we'd run off and left the pup sleeping near the picnic basket. Thank goodness no one had taken her.

Caper licked the woman's face, then curled up in her lap. Mrs. Goads idly stroked her fur, her gaze cemented on Eric emerging from the water. He shook his head in our direction, spraying droplets of water from his hair and causing Mrs. Goads to bury her face in Caper's fur.

A few minutes later, Lowery joined us and let us know they were bringing in divers. "Eric Drake found a patch of gray hair on the dock piling. We fear your husband hit his head, Mrs. Goads. I'm sorry."

A geocache adventure had turned into a possible murder. Which meant the diamonds were buried somewhere around the dock. Unfortunately, yellow crime-scene tape now taunted me and prevented any further investigation.

Suppertime came and went and still no body. Could Mr. Goads have been the one to push his wife, then voluntarily disappeared? That notion was dispelled when a body was dragged from the water at dusk, mere minutes before the search would have been called off.

Mr. Goads had indeed hit his head when he'd fallen in, considering the large goose egg on his forehead. One of the divers said they'd found him tangled in fishing line where the embankment jutted out under the dock.

"Thank you for the comfort of your dog," Mrs. Goads said quietly. "I'm going to go with my husband now." Shoulders slumped, arms again hugging her waist, she shuffled after the men carrying the body.

Just then I noticed the large crowd of spectators gathered on the shore. Some looked sad, but others treated the event as something entertaining. I scowled in the direction of a group of young people, then headed for where we'd left the picnic basket.

Eric joined me a short while later. "The two guys who went hiking haven't returned. I'll have to go looking for them." He rubbed his face with both hands.

"In the dark? Eric, you're exhausted."

"Yes, I am, but they could be in trouble. I'll escort you home before I set out."

"There's no need." I caressed his face. "I know my way. Be careful."

With a grim nod, he jogged down the path, no doubt to get his four-wheeler. His side-by-side was like a golf cart on steroids but couldn't go where the smaller four-wheeler could.

I pulled Caper's leash from the basket. "Okay,

girl. I'm counting on you to give me a warning if someone comes up behind me." Now that the dock was free of law enforcement, I intended to look for whatever had gotten the Goads pushed into the lake.

Doing my best to look like a nosy woman out walking her dog, drawn to the spot of the day's drama, I kept my eyes peeled for trouble. I stepped onto the dock. It floated under my feet, sending a wave of nausea through my stomach. I hated floating docks. When no one shouted for me to get away, I ducked under the crime-scene tape.

Thanks to Mags's influence, I rarely went anywhere without at least a penlight. I clicked it on and shined it around the dock. Where would I stash a geocache?

Nothing on or in the railing, which left the underside. I had no intention of going swimming in the dark. I lay on my belly and scuttled forward, checking each side as far as I could see. Bingo. Attached to the planks on the right-hand side next to a piling was a black, waterproof container. I pulled it free just as Caper started a frenzied bark. Without turning around, I stuffed the box down my shirt.

"A waste of time, girl." I did my best to be convincing for anyone watching. I hooked my hand around Caper's leash. "I have no idea what those people were looking for." As nonchalantly as possible, I stepped off the dock and practically ran for the picnic basket. I dropped the black box inside and raced home.

Back at the house, I darted inside and locked the door, pulling down the shades on my windows. Finished with that, I opened the box. "Oh."

Diamonds sparkled up at me. I'd found the remaining stolen loot. Now where to put it until the authorities could retrieve the jewels? I sent Davis a text and sat on the sofa, my arms wrapped around my knees, trying to figure out what to do now that I had undoubtedly put myself back into a jam.

Instinct told me Caper and I weren't the only ones near the dock. Whoever had hidden the loot in the cache had returned for them, only to find me there.

The radio on my waistband crackled. "Mags here. You there?"

"I'm here."

"There is someone outside of your house again."

My blood froze. "Davis?"

"Nope. Are you alone?"

"Just me and Caper."

My dog lifted her head from her bed and growled.

"Call my cell phone, Mags. I've got a lot to tell you. Out." I shut off the radio and grabbed my cell phone as it rang. I quickly explained all that had happened that day. "The thief saw me find the diamonds. They know I have them."

"Hide."

"There's nowhere to hide in a tiny house."

"Okay. I'm hanging up and calling Davis." Click.

Despite telling Mags there was nowhere to hide, I looked anyway. Just this once, I kind of wished I had a ladder to my bedroom loft instead of stairs. Still, I'd rather be up there than down here. If anyone came after me, they'd get a good kick in the head for their trouble. I scooped up Caper and thundered up the stairs as someone banged on the front door. As the banging continued, I dove under the blankets on my bed. I might be brave when the situation called for it—when I found myself face-to-face with evil—but if I could run and hide, I preferred that option.

My cell phone buzzed. "Open your door in two minutes," Davis texted. "I'll knock three sharp raps."

Relief flooded through me, leaving me limp. I counted to sixty, then crept down the stairs. When three raps sounded on the door, I yelped.

"CJ."

I yanked the door open, slamming it shut behind Davis. "Did you see anyone?"

"There was definitely at least one person on your porch, maybe two. They ran off when I came down the road from Amber's." His sharp gaze studied my face. "Where are they?"

I pointed to the black box on the coffee table.

"You left them in plain sight?"

"I ran upstairs. The diamonds aren't worth my life." If someone had managed to break in, they might have taken the diamonds and left me alone.

"A man was killed over these."

"I don't intend to be."

He opened the box. "I can't tell if this is all of them. No more snooping, CJ. I mean it."

"I'm done. Cross my heart." I tried to look convincing. "It might be too late for me to be completely anonymous, though."

"I agree. Is there anyone who can stay with

you?"

"I'll keep my doors locked at night. I don't need a babysitter."

He didn't look convinced. "Where's Eric?"

"Out searching for missing hikers. I'll have him stay when he returns." I'd done it before. His chivalry prohibited him from taking the bed and leaving me the small sofa, so he folded his long form each night on the makeshift bed too small for him, saying someone would have to get through him to get to me. Since he had a gun and I refused to carry one, it seemed the best situation.

"I'm going to have Lowery stay with you. Maybe she can keep you out of trouble." He headed for the door. "Lock up after me and don't go outside until daylight."

"I won't." I closed the door and locked it, leaning against the raised-paneled wood. *Here we go again.*

When a knock sounded again, I did more than yelp, I screamed.

"CJ?"

I opened the door and threw myself into Eric's arms.

Chapter Eleven

I woke the next morning still wrapped in Eric's arms with my head on his chest. I shifted, trying not to wake him, and shuffled toward the door, a jumping Caper at my feet.

"Don't go out there without me." Eric groaned and stretched. "I love falling asleep with you in my arms, but this sofa leaves aches and pains where I didn't know they could."

"I'm sorry. I kind of acted like a big baby last night."

He unfolded and stood, arching his back. "You've had a lot of pressure the last few days. I think it all caught up with you." He moved forward, as sleek as a lion, and pulled me close. "You're such a brave woman who always looks out for someone else. It's bound to affect you sometimes." He tilted my face to his and kissed me. "Now, let's take the dog out so we can get coffee."

"I never asked whether you found those guys."

"I did. Lost and roaring drunk. They're leaving today, so that's the last we'll have to deal with them." He opened the front door.

Officer Lowery bolted up from where she'd sat on the front porch. "Good morning. I'm happy to say there's nothing new to report."

"How long have you been out here?" I asked.

"About an hour. It's all good. I've got my bag in the car." She hopped to the ground and rushed to a light blue Ford Escort. After rummaging around in a backseat that looked almost as cluttered as Mrs. Schultz's house, she returned with an army-green duffel bag sporting unidentifiable stains.

This didn't bode well for the clean freak in me. "Okay, we're just putting the coffee on." I hooked Caper to her lead and rushed back to the house.

"It will be fine," Eric said. "You'll be safe, I won't have to worry, and you might make a new friend. She seems eager to get to know you better."

"Lucky bag." Lowery held up the duffel when she entered the house. "I'll stash it upstairs."

My eyes widened in horror. "We're sharing a bed?" I whispered.

He shrugged, his amusement growing. "Should be cozy."

I wish my dog had never found that first pouch of diamonds. All I wanted was to live a peaceful life in my tiny house, among the tiny-house community, set beside a lake in the Ozarks. Not too much to ask, was it?

"I took the side nearest the stairs," Lowery said, thundering down the steps. "Anyone who wants you has to get through me."

Her enthusiasm to play bodyguard scared me more than the crook. "God have mercy," I muttered, popping a coffee pod into the Keurig.

Eric gave me a tender kiss behind my ear. "I'll skip the coffee and see you at supper. Don't despair. It's only temporary."

Nodding, I replied, "The faster we catch this jewel thief, the sooner my life gets back to its version of normal."

"At least you have a police officer to keep you out of trouble." He tapped my nose and left me with an over-excited Lowery.

"Remember to call me Ann," Lowery said. "This is much better than the campsite, although I'm starting to feel a little like a nomad with all the moving. If anyone asks, I'm a friend staying with you for a while. Camping wasn't my thing."

I handed her the first cup and watched as she stirred in butter and cinnamon. "What's on the agenda for today? I have to make my rounds every day."

"Not a problem. At the top of my list, which makes it your list, is to make sure Mrs. Schultz is complying with Davis's order to clean out her house."

"I'm pretty sure she hasn't even started."

"Then wear your work clothes, because we'll be cleaning it out for her." She changed from cheerful roommate to stern police officer in the blink of an eye. "I've doughnuts on the table outside. Let's finish breakfast and get this unpleasant business out of the way. Your rounds will have to wait."

I resisted the urge to salute and moved outside.

Caper stared toward the water, the hair on the back of her neck standing at attention.

The stance wasn't lost on Ann. "Somebody's over there your dog doesn't like."

"The person who hit me over the head and kicked her most likely." I stood next to my pup and sipped my coffee. "I hope your purpose here isn't to keep me from finding out the person's identity."

A smile teased at her lips. "My sole purpose is to be your bodyguard. Where you go, I go, unless I'm given an order. Then you follow me."

She might not be my first choice of roommate, but I felt as if Ann might be a kindred spirit. "What made you go into law enforcement?"

"My best friend was abducted walking home from junior high after basketball practice. Her body was found a few days later. She'd been raped and stabbed. I vowed right then that I would do everything in my power to put the bad guys behind bars." She faced me. "What's your story? Why a tiny house?"

"I took care of my grandmother for years until she passed away late last year. I'd gone so long with every day the same that I jumped at the chance to do something different. My first day on the job here, I was told about a rash of burglaries. I've been hooked on the adrenaline rush ever since, despite my tendency to be a big scaredy-cat."

"From what I've heard, you're anything but afraid." She finished her coffee, set it on the picnic table and grabbed a glazed doughnut. "Ready?"

I nodded and grabbed my own sugary breakfast before following her down the road to Mrs.

Schultz's house. Since belongings now sat on the minuscule porch, I got the impression she'd added to her hoard rather than diminished.

Cop face still in place, Ann knocked on the door. "Police, open up."

Mrs. Schultz came around the corner. "Something wrong?"

"Ma'am, on the orders of the fire department, Detective Davis has sent me here to clean out your house. CJ and I would like to get started immediately." She flashed her badge, then handed me a paper mask and gloves from her pants pocket.

Looking as if we'd told her we had to take her dog, she squeezed past us and inched open the door. "There's no room for all of us."

"We'll take everything out one at a time and set it on the lawn," Ann said. "You may go through everything, but any garbage must be thrown away." She took a plastic chair from the porch and set it on the grass. "You sit here and let us do the work."

I sent Tammy a text asking her to come and clean the house later before we put things back in. She replied she was free in an hour and would help Mrs. Schultz sort.

A rotten smell drifted from inside the house, causing me to quickly don my mask. Moments later, Ann handed me a box, then another and another. I heard things falling as she dug.

"Be careful." Mrs. Schultz's face darkened. "Those are my treasures."

No response came from Ann other than yet another box. Then she started handing me random items not packed away. Clothes, dishes, plastic flowers. When everything was out, she grabbed a broom and swept the garbage and expired foods into a pile. The woman was a workhorse.

"CJ., Please check the fridge and stove. I have a horrible feeling that whatever is causing the foul odor is still in here."

Oh, gross. I opened the fridge to see it full of expired food, but thankfully no maggots. A box of insulin sat on top of a container of expired eggs—nothing a good scrubbing wouldn't take care of. The miniature stove and oven was a whole other story. "There's an entire rotted chicken in the oven." I gagged.

"Throw it in a garbage bag. Anything gone bad in the fridge, too." Ann left the things in a pile and stormed outside. "Mrs. Schultz, what's up with the expired food? It isn't healthy. We cannot have your home deteriorate to this state again."

I peered out the door to watch the battle of the wills.

Ann picked up a bent aluminum pan. "This is trash. Broken items and duplicates must go. If they're in good condition, we'll hold a yard sale. I wish you understood the severity of the situation. Do you want to be kicked out and made homeless? You wouldn't be able to take any of this with you."

The woman nodded and tossed the pan into the trash pile. "Don't forget to look in the floor storage. I've managed to squirrel quite a bit of things in there."

I turned and searched for a fingerhold in the floor. Where there had once been a pull, only a hole remained, covered up with papers. I pulled the door up and stared into what was probably the only things in good condition in the house. Folded clothes, a jewelry box, makeup. She'd filled her storage and every room until there was no room for her.

"Everything in the floor looks good," I yelled out the door. "Want me to bring the things out?"

"Yes." Ann's voice left no room for argument. "Every single thing must come out."

It wasn't until I emptied the space that something caught my attention. Wedged in a crack sparkled a sapphire ring. Since I wore gloves, I pried it out and carried it to the women. "Is this yours, Mrs. Schultz?" If it was real, it looked as if it was worth a fortune.

She peered at the ring. "Oh, I found that a few days ago. Thank you for finding it."

Ann held out her hand. "This looks like one of the missing pieces of stolen jewelry. Where did you find it?"

"Near that old log people like to sit on by the water. I'd like that to go in the keep pile."

"We need to determine whether it's stolen property, Mrs. Schultz. Same as before, if it isn't part of the stolen items, you'll get it back."

Had the person who'd hit me in the head missed the ring when they retrieved the pouch? Could there be anything else hidden in there? I glanced in that direction, itching to explore. Every piece of located jewelry convinced me the thief resided in the campground.

Ann followed my gaze and nodded, tacitly saying she agreed with me. "We'll discuss this later." She dropped the ring into the pocket of her loose-fitting cargo pants.

Tammy arrived with a bucket of cleaning supplies and marched inside to tackle the cleaning, leaving the arguing with Mrs. Schultz over every item to myself and Ann. My stomach growled, reminding me I hadn't had anything to eat but a doughnut, and lunchtime was hours ago.

"I'm ordering pizza." I placed the order on my cell phone and got back to work sorting trash from treasure. As I worked, I mulled over the happenings of the days since the jewelry-store heist.

First, Caper showed herself a finder of diamonds; I was attacked; a couple was pushed into the water for being too close to a cache, and now Mrs. Schultz had a ring. I eyed the growing pile of jewelry at her feet and couldn't help but wonder if all of it was stolen. What if the thief had hidden behind the pleasant face of an old woman? Being a hoarder gave her the perfect hiding place. No one wanted to venture inside her house.

I motioned Ann over. "I think you should compare the list of missing items to those." I pointed to Mrs. Schultz's stash.

"You're brilliant, CJ." Ann pulled up some photos on her phone and started comparing. By the time she finished, five items of jewelry had been declared stolen. "Mrs. Schultz, I'm taking you to the station for questioning in regard to the jewelry-store theft."

"I found all that." Her face paled. "I swear."

"In a glass case, perhaps?"

"I have an alibi." She struggled to her feet.

"You can explain all of that to us at the station. CJ, you'll have to come with me."

"What about all my things?" Mrs. Schultz said, her eyes welling with tears.

"I'll go through them and throw away the trash," Tammy offered from the open front door. "I'll bring the boxes inside and help her sort through them when she returns."

Excellent idea. I doubted Mrs. Schultz was the thief, but she might know more about everything than she knew.

Chapter Twelve

Milton glanced up in surprise from the bullpen when Ann led me and Mrs. Schultz into the station. "Don't tell me you've solved the case after living with CJ for fewer than twenty-four hours."

Ann shook her head. "No, but I might have gotten us our first solid lead." She helped the distraught Mrs. Schultz into a chair in a small interrogation room, then took a seat opposite Mrs. Schultz at a battered metal table, leaving me to pull up a chair beside her. Ann folded her hands on the table. "It's quite a coincidence that you've managed to stumble upon several pieces of the missing jewelry."

Milton joined us, crossing his arms and leaning against the wall. "This ought to be interesting."

"I go for walks and look in, under, and between everything. You never know what you might find." The poor thing twisted the hem of her blouse with her hands.

"If you're as innocent as you claim, what's the alibi you say you have?" Ann's face could have been carved from stone.

"I was getting a slice of pie at the diner."

"The diner that happens to be across the street from the jewelry store?"

Her eyes widened. "The town isn't that big. Everything is close by."

True. Ann would have to find more to go on if she wanted to convict Mrs. Schultz.

"You must have seen something on your rambling quests," Ann said. "Think. Without other evidence, you are our main person of interest."

"Oh, mercy." Mrs. Schultz exhaled. "Give me a minute. I tend to be so focused on what I'm doing, I rarely notice what goes on around me."

"You'd better start," Milton said, playing an even badder cop than Ann.

Tears ran freely down Mrs. Schultz's face by this time. "I saw CJ's dog. She gets around as much as I do, but I guess a dog isn't a suspect."

"No, ma'am," Ann said.

She proceeded to describe all the people she'd noticed walking along the lake's edge. A whole lot of people, considering she didn't pay attention to what went on around her. Lies or confusion? It didn't help clear her of guilt. "Oh, I saw someone in baggy clothes and a hat leaning over the dock early one evening."

"Before or after the drowning?" Milton barked.

"Before?"

"Is that a question?"

She shook her head. "No, I did see someone. I

think." Yes, clearly confused a lot of the time, poor thing.

"That's where I found the cache," I volunteered, trying to give Mrs. Schultz time to compose herself. "I think someone watched me get it, then came to my house the night Mr. Goads drowned."

Ann exhaled sharply through her nose. "We'll take you home, Mrs. Schultz, but let me advise you not to leave town."

It was a quiet ride home. Tammy hadn't yet started sorting, so we left Mrs. Schultz to finish what we'd started, and then headed back to my place to get the golf cart. "I don't think she's the thief," I said as we headed for the other side of the lake.

"Neither do I." Ann sighed. "But she's a tight-lipped woman. The only way we'd get any information out of her was to scare her a little. I hated doing it, but I didn't see an alternative."

"Now what?"

"I have no idea. Keep looking, I guess."

"What in the world?" My mouth fell open. Mags on crutches, Rose at her side, hobbled down the curving road that circled the campsites. I should have known there was no keeping that woman down. I stopped beside them. "Get in, you crazy old fool."

"Thanks. I'm getting blisters in my armpits." Mags took the passenger seat while Ann climbed onto the small backseat with Rose.

"What are you doing out?" I glared first at her, then over my shoulder at Rose.

"I couldn't stay cooped up after seeing you and

Officer Lowery haul Mrs. Schultz away, now could I? Then, when you brought her home, we skedaddled over here to do some snooping." Mags gave a sly grin. "Bringing her back meant she isn't our thief, right?"

You're incorrigible, and you shouldn't spy on people. It's rude." I pressed the gas pedal, having no idea where to go or what to look for. Par for the course.

"I get bored. Since I've seen the person outside your house a few times," Mags added, "I feel like I'm a good judge as to body shape and the way the person moves. So, we need to get everyone up and moving. How about a great big cookout? A summer celebration."

"That might work," Ann said from the back. "It would reinforce the idea that I'm nothing more than CJ's friend, which in theory, might not prevent the thief from making an attempt to shut her up. At that point, I'd nab them."

I liked the idea of a summer bash but not of being bait, which is what it sounded like to me. "There's not enough money in the budget. I spent it for the barbeque."

"Put up a flier, make it a potluck, and call it a day. That's how things used to be done."

"I don't know," Ann said. "It might be too dangerous. Someone is already stalking CJ."

"Yeah." Rose turned and leaned over the seat. "What if someone slips poison into CJ's plate?"

"Thanks for that unpleasant thought," I said, parking in front of Robinson's trailer. "Let's go over what we know. The suspect wear Keds, either a man's small foot or a woman's large, stores diamonds around like a squirrel hides nuts, and has no qualms about killing someone...remember Mr. Goads? We really don't know much, do we?"

"Mrs. Schultz's beginning signs of dementia bother me," Ann said. "I still think the woman knows more than she thinks she does. She needs to get rattled up in order to remember."

Mags frowned at her. "No, she needs a gentle nudging. Badgering the poor thing will only make her more confused. Shame on you." She tapped me on the arm. "Take me home. I'm going to bake the woman a casserole."

A commotion near the restrooms drew my attention. "It'll have to wait. Duty calls." I sped toward the loud voices.

The women from site 101 and Frank Dickson faced off in front of the door to the women's restroom. "You, sir, are a pervert." Ioda gave him a two-handed shove.

"No." He held up his hands. "I simply got the wrong door. Look. The painted signs are faded."

So they were. I made a mental note to send Roy over to fix them. When Ann started to climb from the cart, I stopped her. "A friend, remember?" I approached the group. "No harm done, ladies. Mr. Dickson, go on ... to your site." I started to say home, he'd been there so long.

"Of course, there's harm done. He was inside while Carol took a shower." Ioda planted her fists on her hips.

"I did my business and left." He rubbed his chin. "I did wonder why there were no urinals, but I had a lot to drink last night, and, well—" He shrugged.

"Then what were you doing rummaging through the trashcan outside the door?" Carol tilted her head. "Suspicious behavior, if you ask me."

Myrna, who had been quiet during all this, said, "Maybe you're the one who pushed that man into the lake. Maybe you had too much to drink then, too."

His brows lowered. "What in the world are you talking about?"

"You didn't know someone drowned yesterday?" I raised my brows.

"I wasn't here yesterday. I went to town to stock up on supplies." He glanced from one woman to the other. "You aren't going to pin anything on me except a stupid mistake." He whirled and stormed away.

In my opinion, it was time for the whole lot to give up camping and go back to where they came from. "Is that all?"

The women nodded and strolled back to their site, towels slung over their arms. I shook my head at the continuing drama and returned to the cart.

"Did you see the size of their feet?" Mags asked. "At least a woman's nine. All three of them."

"But I've been in their tent and not seen a pair of Keds, nothing but sandals," I said.

"Did you go through their boxes and bags?"

"Well, no."

"Okay then."

"This proves nothing," Ann said, the voice of reason. "We'll keep an eye on them and Mr.

Dickson. He has a criminal past."

"I've been arrested for shoplifting." Rose scowled. "Doesn't mean I'm the guilty one this time."

I leaned my head on the steering wheel. What was I missing?

Mags rubbed my back. "Maybe you should rest. This seems a bit much for you."

"I'm fine." I shrugged her off and sped back toward the community, pleased to see Mrs. Schultz's yard free of boxes, and tables lined up piled with things for a yard sale. I stopped so Ann could inspect and hopefully approve the progress.

When Ann hopped from the back of the cart, I followed, leaving Mags and Rose to browse among the items for sale.

"Wow." The inside of Mrs. Schultz's home sparkled. "This is a different house." It still contained a lot of things, but so did Mags's.

"Good job, Mrs. Schultz," Ann said with a smile. "How does it feel?"

"Very freeing." She folded, then rolled a dishtowel and put it in a basket on a shelf above the sink. "Tammy gave me some great organizing tips, too. I can have more things if they're organized, you know. Not like that person stashing diamonds everywhere."

Ann and I glanced at each other. "Do you remember something?" Ann asked.

"About what, dear?"

Ann face-palmed herself and groaned. "It's right there on the edge of her brain."

"Doesn't that worry you?" I asked in a low

voice. "If the thief thinks Mrs. Schultz knows something, she might become a target like I am."

"I'm not worried, CJ." A spark of awareness came into the old woman's eyes. "I remembered something. More than one person gathered together, whispering in the shadows. Unfortunately, I couldn't tell whether they were male or female, but I'm leaning toward female. Their bodies were rather slim."

Ann gave the woman a hug. "You are remarkable."

"Why?" And the confusion returned.

Back outside, I voiced the concerns riddling me. "Is she self-sufficient enough to live alone?"

"I was thinking the same thing. I'm going to ask Davis whether we can get a day nurse who's certified to carry a gun. That way we can keep Mrs. Schultz safe." Her gaze wandered across the lake. "The suspect will be coming for both of you."

Chapter Thirteen

When Eric showed up the next morning with coffee and pastries, he agreed with Ann that Mrs. Schultz and I were in imminent danger. "You're getting close to another face-to-face confrontation. I'm glad you're here, Ann. With summer upon us, I'm kept too busy to stay at CJ's side." A crooked smile spread across his face. "Although there's no place I'd rather be. But I'm keeping my eyes and ears open to any news about the thieves."

The morning seemed too pleasant for such a dark cloud to hover over me. If the thief had only left my dog alone, I'd have been happy to stay in my safe little world and not get involved. I sighed. Why couldn't my life be less...exciting? Oh sure, after the boredom of the last few years caring for Grams, I'd wanted—prayed—for something more. I didn't expect that to include thieves and murderers.

"What's on your mind, sweetheart?" Concern

etched lines between Eric's brow.

"I didn't expect any of this when I wished for adventure. I thought I'd simply get a change of pace, a new home and job." I stared into my cup.

"Life often doesn't turn out as we'd thought," Ann said. "From what I've heard from Milton and Davis, they might not have caught the killer a while back if not for your bravery and tenacity."

"Really?" I met her gaze. "I thought I was more of a nuisance."

She laughed. "You're a civilian. You aren't supposed to be smarter than they are. It bruises their ego."

"I don't feel smart or brave. I hid under my covers when someone banged on my door, and I have no idea where to proceed from here."

Eric wrapped his arm around my shoulders. "It isn't your job. You'll do more than enough by staying aware of what's going on around you. Maybe you can help Mrs. Schultz stay in reality so she can tell us more of what she knows."

"I can do that." My mood brightened. "She reminds me of Grams. I have experience to help her." Why hadn't I thought of that? Because I'd grown selfish being on my own, that's why. "I'll go check on her after breakfast."

Ann sobered. "I have a dentist appointment. Can you promise me not to do anything stupid while I'm gone? Maybe stay inside with Mrs. Schultz? I can ask Roy to drive by once in a while."

"Sure, but I do have to make my rounds. I was hoping to take Mrs. Schultz with me. She might see something that jogs her memory."

"No," Ann and Eric said in unison.

"Not until I get back," Ann added. "I mean it, CJ. I'll put you in jail for the day if I have to."

I rolled my eyes. "Davis is always threatening to do that."

"I'm not threatening." Uh oh, her bad-cop face was back. No promises. I'd take Mags and her Taser along with us. No one would bother three people. Strength in numbers, right?

Eric groaned and stood. "She's not listening to a word you're saying, Ann."

"I am." I frowned. "I'm listening to every word."

"There's a difference between listening and hearing." He gave me a quick kiss. "Please make wise choices. I'll be back as soon as I can."

"I'll cook grilled salmon for supper."

He chuckled. "You mean I'll grill it."

"Sure, but I'll fix everything else." I grinned, more than happy to change the subject. I might do some snooping, ask a few questions, but I wouldn't put myself in harm's way. The reminder that harm had recently come looking for me sent a shiver of caution up my spine. I was smarter this time and not going anywhere alone, even my own home since Eric insisted on following me to Mrs. Schultz's house.

I approached her front door and blew him a kiss before knocking. He grabbed the kiss, closed his hand, and held his fist to his heart before driving away. I grinned like a lovesick freshman and rapped on the door.

Mrs. Schultz peered out through an inch-wide

opening. "Hello?"

"It's me, CJ. I'm here to see whether you'd like to take a ride with me."

She narrowed her eyes. "I don't ride with strangers."

"I'm not a stranger. I helped you clean your house, remember?" My smile trembled. What if I couldn't help her? I recognized the same signs Grams had experienced. Confusion, forgetfulness, paranoia.

"Oh yes. I know you." She stepped back and opened the door. "That other woman made me get rid of all my things. She's not as nice as you, Tammy."

"Uh, I'm CJ." The house did look nice and clean. Organized.

"Right. You're the mean one. No." She tapped her forefinger against her lips. "The cop is the mean one."

"Right." I grinned. "Let's go for a ride. You can hold my dog."

"I like dogs." She grabbed a floppy hat from a hook on the wall, looped her arm through a large matching bag, and strolled out the door. By the time I joined her, she was in the passenger seat with Caper on her lap, both looking content.

Next stop, Mags, who wasn't pleased that another woman sat in what she considered her seat. "This is not the first time I've been relegated to the back," she said.

"Sorry, but Mrs. Schultz is older."

"You might as well call me Doris, dear." Mrs. Schultz smiled. "If we're going to be friends, we should be on a first-name basis."

"Ready for an adventure?" I asked, pulling away from Mags's house.

"Yes." She leaned her crutches next to her and turned to face forward as much as the smaller seat would allow. "So, what's the plan?"

"We'll drive around and hope Doris remembers something."

"Remember what?" Doris rubbed Caper's ears.

"So, we're trying to rattle some rocks," Mags said. "This ought to be fun. Okay, Doris, point out anyone who looks like the diamond thief."

Doris scrunched her lips. "I never saw their faces when they came by my house last night."

I whipped around to face her. "What?"

"I saw someone outside keeping to the shadows. At first I thought it was the girl who helps Mags, but this person was bigger."

Now we were getting somewhere. "What else do you remember?"

She tapped her finger against her lips again. "Not fat, thin, but not skinny. Long hair, I think."

"A woman?"

"If it was, she wasn't blessed in the chest department." Doris gave a sly smile and kept gazing straight ahead. "I'd like to visit that chapel everyone is always talking about."

"Sure, we can go there first." I was always happy to share what I considered one of my greatest accomplishments—renovating the fallen-down chapel. The cross that lit up at night had saved my life when someone tried to kill me. I'd literally blinded them by its light.

I parked the cart and stayed close by Mags's side as she hobbled down the dirt path while using only one of her crutches. "You should stay in the cart."

"Not a chance. Last time I did that, a tree almost fell on me and Caper."

"Then at least use both crutches. It won't take me but a minute to go back and get the other one."

"Fine." She leaned against a tree. "Make it snappy. Doris went on ahead—not a smart thing when you're a threat to someone."

Agreed. I jogged back to the cart and grabbed the crutch. We wouldn't catch up to Doris, but we could go a little faster.

"Do you think she'll remember anything useful?" Mags glanced at me. "She seems to get worse every day. Maybe you should give her a ride to the doctor for some tests."

"That's a good idea." I opened the door to the chapel and let Mags enter before me.

Doris sat in the first pew, staring at the simple wooden cross hanging on the wall behind the pulpit. "It's peaceful here."

I sat next to her. "This is one of my favorite places. Before we fixed it up, a killer camped in here."

"That's an interesting story." She put a hand to her chest. "I'm afraid I won't be able to help you today. The ticker doesn't seem to be working right since that nice nurse gave me a shot."

"What?" I hadn't noticed until then how clammy her skin had become. "Mags, call Amber, then an ambulance." I'd seen Amber's car at her house, so she didn't work that day. "Who gave you a shot, Doris?"

"Someone gave me a shot?" Her eyes widened in horror. "Where am I?"

"Amber will be here in five minutes," Mags said. "Heart attack?"

"She said someone gave her a shot." I rolled up the sleeve of her blouse. A tiny red dot showed the site of the injection. By now, Doris's breathing had become erratic.

By the time Amber arrived, Doris had slumped over. I explained what little I knew, then stepped back and let a real nurse take over.

When Amber had taken the vitals and the ambulance arrived, she sat in the pew. "I'm the only nurse living at Heavenly Acres. Do you think Doris is confused? Maybe she got the shot at home. Is she diabetic?"

I remembered the insulin in her refrigerator. "Yes, why?"

"Maybe she gave herself too much insulin? It can mimic a heart attack."

"Why don't you stop yapping and go see if the fake nurse left a clue." Mags sat down, her crutches clattering against the wood of the pew.

With Doris in the capable hands of paramedics on her way to the hospital, a little sleuthing wouldn't hurt. If she had indeed given herself too much insulin, she could no longer live alone. The State would insist she go into assisted living. I'd hate for that to happen if someone had tried to harm her rather than her being absentminded.

It didn't make sense to me that someone would

carry around a syringe in case they ran into Doris, or me, since we were both an obvious threat. Unless the person was a diabetic, so they carried syringes around with them. Hmm. "What about an EpiPen? Could it cause the same symptoms? It makes more sense that someone would have it on their person."

Amber grinned. "You're brilliant."

I pushed open the back door and studied the ground at the bottom of the two cement steps. Footprints led into the woods, but I wasn't a good enough tracker to know how fresh they were. The chapel was open to anyone seeking peace.

"Those were made today," Amber said. "Except I can't tell when. The ground is too dry."

"Are we going with the notion that someone tried to harm Doris?"

She nodded. "The needle hole was fresh. The blood hadn't clotted yet. I'm calling Davis."

Poor Doris. I hoped she wouldn't become the first victim of a killer.

While we waited for Davis, who said he'd come himself this time, I thought over what Doris had said. More and more I leaned toward a female thief. Doris seemed the type to assume a nurse was a woman, especially if she wasn't wearing scrubs and said she was one. Did that mean that one of the ladies camping at site 101 had followed us? Or maybe one of the women from the tiny-house community? Several of them fit the description of being small chested with big feet.

I put Dickson at the bottom of my so-called suspect list and decided to spend a little more time getting to know the women around me. Mags's idea of a barbeque would be a good place to start. I'd be their friend first, then once they grew comfortable around me, I'd start digging into their lives. Time was running out. Robinson would be returning, and it would look too suspicious for me to be at the campground every day like now.

"What are you thinking?" Amber narrowed her eyes.

"Time to make some friends."

Chapter Fourteen

I called the hospital the next morning to check on Doris and was told she had, indeed, been given too much epinephrine, but would be fine after a few days recuperation. If we hadn't been there to help her, she could have died. Now, it was time to pay a visit to the Rowes in number ten and talk about fragrance.

Of course, Ann came with me, despite having a tooth pulled the day before. "Not letting anyone shoot you up with drugs," she mumbled around gauze.

I shook my head and put Caper in the middle of the seat. I'd pay close attention to how my dog behaved as I visited the women on my list. Caper might be friendly, but I had the impression she wasn't a fan of the person who had stuck her in the canoe and hit me over the head. "You growl when we find those bad guys, okay? Show the world that smart and mighty can come in a small package." I ruffled the hair on top of her head before climbing in the driver's seat. "I'll be fine. I don't plan on leaving the community for at least an hour. You should rest during that time."

She shook her head, cupping her right jaw. "Drive."

Which took all of two minutes. "They'd be more susceptible to answering questions if I was alone."

"I'm just a friend, remember." She slid from the cart. "Maybe I want a new fragrance, too."

Sighing, I scooped up Caper and marched to the front door. Mike Rowe answered before I knocked.

"Good morning, ladies." He smiled but didn't move aside for us to enter. "What can I do for you?"

"We'd like to design a fragrance." I grinned, standing on my tiptoes to see in the house.

"There isn't much room, but I guess we can squeeze you in." He frowned and let us enter.

Kim stood over several vials next to the tiny sink. Without looking up, she said, "There are forms on the wall. Fill them out to give me some kind of idea what you like. Then we can have fun."

Considering they weren't making me feel exactly welcomed, fun wouldn't be part of the experience. Wasn't this their job? Then why act as if we were intruding? I bent to put Caper down.

"No way." Kim glanced over and glared. "The dog stays outside. I don't want her hair in my vials." She made a shooing motion with her hands.

Caper growled and snapped, obviously thinking the woman planned on hitting me.

"Shh, it's okay." I stepped outside and hooked

her leash to the porch railing. "You can keep guard out here." After a quick glance across the lake to see if I could catch a glimpse of Eric, I didn't see him, so I returned inside where Ann was at the sink with Kim. Good. I could do some observing with the other women occupied and Mike bent over a laptop on a pull-down desk.

Pretending to think hard about my selections of floral, woody, or musk, I studied the room through lowered lashes. Boxes still sat piled just about everywhere they could be, but most now seemed to be in the loft, giving more space downstairs. Still we were cramped. Dishes were minimal. These two didn't seem the type to entertain anyway. A cookstove sat on top of the fridge to be pulled down when needed. I didn't see anything that could tell me whether these two were our jewel thieves. I needed an opportunity to go through all those boxes.

"What's in the boxes?" Uh-oh. Hadn't meant to say that out loud.

"We already told you it's our supplies." Mike narrowed his eyes. "Why so nosy?"

"A lot of supplies to bring on vacation." I shrugged.

"We still have orders to fill." He rolled his eyes and returned to his laptop.

"But why here?"

He exhaled slowly. "Our house is being renovated. This place is better than a motel room."

Ignoring Ann's look of warning, I persisted. "Is there much money in designing fragrances?"

Mike sighed again and swiveled in his chair to

face me. "I can see I'm not going to get any work done as long as you're here. We do alright. I did say we were renovating, right? That isn't exactly cheap."

"Some people choose nefarious means to get more money. Did you hear about the jewel theft?" I widened my eyes in what I hoped was a look of innocence. "That took some guts, didn't it?"

His face darkened. "Are you accusing us of something?"

"No." I put a hand to my chest. "Just making conversation until it's my turn."

"Well, don't. I have too much work to chitchat." He turned away.

Ann gave me a look of exasperation. "I apologize for my talkative friend," she mumbled. "She isn't a fan of silence."

Actually I was, but not when I had a mystery to solve. I glanced at the boxes again, starting to feel as if I were scaling the wrong mountain. The Rowes appeared to be exactly who they said they were, and I sat there committed to spending a hundred dollars on a custom fragrance.

When my turn came, I chose something mysteriously floral as Kim called it. I rather liked the way it smelled after she blended everything together. Hopefully, Eric would, too.

"I don't think they're our culprits," Ann said when we were back in the cart.

"Me neither." I'd focus on the three women on an extended camping trip. "I still want to see inside their boxes, though."

"No way to do that legally unless they allow it."

She rested her head against the seat. "What's your plan for the rest of the day?"

"Same old thing. Check out the campground, ask questions—"

"Get yourself killed."

"Hopefully not." I grinned and stopped in front of Mags's house. She'd never forgive me if I left the community without her.

"I thought you'd forgotten about me," she said as Ann moved to the back of the cart.

"Never." As we drove, I explained why we'd dropped the Rowes off our suspect list to focus elsewhere.

"That Frank Dickson has been nosing around Heavenly Acres all morning," she said. "I'm surprised you didn't see him."

That got both my and Ann's attention. "What was he doing?" Ann said, spitting out her gauze.

"Walking up and down the road, looking at all the houses. He stopped next to the playground like some pedophile, watched the kids play for a while, then moved on. Last I saw him he was headed in the direction of the chapel."

So we headed in that direction. I stopped shy of the path leading to the door. Through the glass, we watched Dickson searching for something.

"That's not suspicious behavior at all," Mags said.

"Looks perfectly innocent." Ann leaned over the seat.

"Maybe he's looking for the rest of the diamonds," I added. "If he were the thief, he'd know where they were. Maybe he found out that not all the diamonds have been accounted for."

"The only way he'd know that is if someone talked about it." Mags grabbed her crutch. "Let's go ask him who he overheard."

Ann put a hand on her shoulder. "No, let's observe him for a day or two. Right now while he's occupied, let's go search his site. If anyone asks, I didn't advise this; in fact, I told you not to and went along to stop you."

I laughed and circled the cart around. "Davis will never buy that excuse. It might work if you were with anyone but me and Mags."

"It's the one I'll stick to."

I parked the cart in front of Robinson's trailer, and we walked to site 107 in case we needed to make a quick getaway. I tied Caper to a tree to give us a warning if anyone approached.

"I'll stay out here," Ann said, sitting at the picnic table. "I'm not jeopardizing my career any more than I already have. If Dickson comes up, I'll say I took a break because of the pain in my jaw, which isn't far from the truth."

I had a strong suspicion that the rookie would be in trouble for just knowing about us going into the man's tent, but kept my opinion to myself. She was the law enforcement, not me.

Mags stood in the center of the tent and turned in a slow, hobbling circle. "I can't hear anything from outside, so he didn't overhear a conversation from inside the tent."

"The sites are far enough apart that you wouldn't hear a normal conversation even outside. He had to have been walking by. The question is where. I doubt there are any clues in here, but we should look. Make it quick." I wanted to get back to the chapel and explore some myself after Dickson left.

Other than ice chests full of beer and piles of dirty clothes under his cot, we found nothing to suggest the man was a thief or murderer. I glanced at a pair of muddy shoes sticking out from under a lawn chair. Man's size eleven, which was a woman's size nine, right? But they were Keds and our resident shoe expert, Rose, had insisted we were looking for Keds.

"He's not our suspect, but he was definitely looking for something."

Mags agreed, and I told Ann my thoughts when we returned to the cart. "I need to change my patrolling this side of the lake to the evening," I said. "I'll walk it rather than drive, and maybe I'll overhear something."

"As long as I'm with you, I don't care what time you go." Ann gave me a look that clearly said she wouldn't argue the fact.

We passed Dickson returning as we headed back, nodded and waved as if everything was normal. He returned the gesture, but the scowl remained on his face.

"The old buzzard," Mags huffed. "He could at least smile."

"I'm guessing he didn't find what he was looking for," I said. Good. Maybe we'd find something. "If you overheard something that made you think to look at the chapel, you'd also search around the cross, right? I wonder if he thought of that."

"Go there first," Ann said. "The way your mind works is scary."

"I've heard that before. Is Dickson far enough away not to see us?"

"Yes," Ann answered. "Unless he's hiding in the trees, and why would he do that unless he suspects us of suspecting him of something?"

"He ain't that bright." Mags climbed from the cart and, leaving her crutches behind, and hobbled toward the cross. "I'm no Daniel Boone, but the ground doesn't look as if anyone has been here in a day or two."

I agreed. The leaves that always stayed a little damp under the thick canopy of tree branches didn't seem as disturbed as they would if someone had disturbed them. I nudged a few aside with my toe to confirm the ground underneath was damp. "Let's start looking for hidden treasure."

We each took a different section of the area around the cross. I chose the backside where the solar panel was. I'd have to have Roy clear away more of the brush, or better yet, put the panel higher to reach the sun since I'd noticed it didn't seem as bright last night. I cleared debris and found nothing.

Straightening, I surveyed a few feet from the cross wishing for the proverbial X that marked the location of treasure. Keeping my gaze on the ground, I took ten steps forward and halted at the base of a tree with a split high in the branches. That's where I'd hide something. I stood on my tiptoes to reach for the lowest branch.

"CJ," Ann hissed. "Time to go."

The urgency in her voice had me rushing to the cart. "What happened?"

"Someone who doesn't want us to hear them coming is coming."

Chapter Fifteen

"I don't want to leave then." I shook my head. "That almost certainly means they've come to retrieve something. We should hide and spy on them."

"Stop wasting time and hide this cart." Mags slid out and grabbed her crutches. By the time Ann and I followed, she was hunkered down in the bushes near the chapel.

Myrna wandered into view, stopping now and then to study a plant. Sometimes, she'd pull it from the ground and put it in the pocket of her full skirt.

"It looks like she's gathering leaves," I said. "There's nothing suspicious about that." I glared at Ann. "As a police officer, you shouldn't be so quick to jump to conclusions."

She shrugged, a contrite look on her face. "Blame it on my rookie status." She straightened and brushed dried grass from her pant legs. "Let's go."

"Nope. I'm staying right here until she leaves. I'm finding those diamonds." I sat cross-legged on the ground. "I'm starting to get bored doing the same thing day after day with no end in sight." I did want to talk to Myrna and her friends. Also I wanted to find out who Dickson had overheard talking. I sighed and pushed to my feet. Sitting there wasn't going to accomplish anything.

To prevent Myrna from accidentally stumbling across the loot, I stepped from my hiding place and acted surprised to see her. "Hello." I smiled.

"Hello." Her smile seemed forced. "I'm not breaking any rules, am I?" She glanced around me to where Ann approached us. "No law against picking foliage?"

"Not that I know of." I tilted my head. "Have you noticed any strangers around the campgrounds? Anyone that looks as if they don't belong?"

"I don't associate with any of them, so I wouldn't know. I stay with my friends and my leather work mostly."

"Have you sold many leather pouches?"

Her eyes narrowed. "Is this an interrogation?"

I lifted one shoulder. "Several have been found here and there. I'm wondering whether they're yours."

"I hope people who buy my items care a little more than to leave them lying around." She plucked some moss from a tree.

Caper bounded toward us. At the sight of Myrna, she stopped and barked.

"I don't think my dog likes you much since you tied her up." I lifted my eyebrows.

"She tried to bite me. I don't like dogs anyway. Noisy, smelly creatures."

"Animals are a great judge of character," Mags said.

Myrna shook her head and strode past us, muttering something about people minding their own business. She yelped and jumped as Caper nipped at her ankle. "See? That dog is a menace." She stared at Caper for a minute, her eyes wide, before turning and leaving.

Hmm. I agreed with Mags. Animals were a good judge of character. Once Myrna was out of sight, I turned to Ann. "What do you think?"

Her gaze transferred from the path the other woman had taken to me. "We need to look a bit more at the ladies of site 101." She pulled her cell phone from her pocket and moved a few steps away. When she hung up, she said, "I've asked Milton to run a background check on all three of them, plus Dickson."

I rubbed my hands together. "I like focusing on four instead of many. We'll work on marking them off our list one-by-one. Then we're bound to catch our man or woman."

"You sure went from grumpy to happy fast," Mags said. "Are we going to continue searching for the diamonds or stand around yakking all day?"

We decided to search until growling stomachs sent us home. If there'd been anything out there, it was well hidden or had already been removed. I figured the latter. What better ploy to steer us away from the truth than to run us off, gather the treasure, then appear to do nothing more than wander the forest?

As we entered the community, Daniel and Rose were sitting on the playground swings. The two seemed to be deep in conversation. I honked the horn and they glanced up. With grins on both faces, they sprinted toward us.

"Guess what?" Daniel crossed his arms and took a wide-legged stance.

"No time for guessing, boy," Mags said. "Tell us what you know."

He rolled his eyes. "Rose and I have been doing a bit of snooping around the campgrounds and we heard the man at site 107 telling someone on the phone that he might know where they could get their hands on enough money to set them up for life."

"When did you hear this?"

"Just a few minutes ago."

"It isn't safe for the two of you to get involved." Ann adopted her cop face.

He glanced at Rose. "Summers are boring. It doesn't take me all day to mow."

"Mags doesn't need me anymore," Rose added, "so what am I supposed to do?"

"Help your mother watch the other children," Ann suggested.

I knew from experience that Ann was wasting her breath. These two teenagers would do what they wanted. "Be careful, okay?" I drove home, offering to make egg salad sandwiches for us.

Instead, Eric sat at the picnic table with several bags of hamburgers and fries. I grinned and rushed into his arms. "I don't get to see you nearly enough now that vacation time is here." I wrapped my arms around his waist and rested my head on his chest.

He chuckled. "That's why I brought lunch. Your stomach is better than any clock. Come eat and tell me what you three have been up to."

So, we did. "Want me to dig around the chapel? I might see something you ladies missed."

"If you have time, that would be great." I popped a french fry in my mouth. "We're going to question the three friends, do some snooping when the sun goes down, but other than that we've hit a cement wall."

"It will all click into place eventually. You have a police officer helping you this time."

"I don't know any more than CJ does," Ann said. "I thought solving a crime was merely following clues, and maybe it is. Our problem is we have few clues to follow. Of course, my orders are to be a bodyguard to CJ, not actually try to solve the case." She took a bite of her burger, swallowed, and continued. "If Davis finds out, he'll fire me. At the very least, I'll receive a reprimand."

"What will you do if you lose your job?" I didn't want to be the cause of her getting fired.

"Maybe I'll become a professional bodyguard." She wiggled her eyebrows. "I'm definitely getting the practice."

"No one has bothered me since you arrived," I said. I had no reason to believe anyone knew her to be anything more than a friend, but most criminals preferred to harass one person, not several.

Eric tossed his wadded napkin into the bag in front of him. "Davis won't fire you. He knows CJ well enough not to be fooled into thinking she wouldn't involve you. What he might be upset about is your lack of professionalism if you do anything illegal."

"Nope. Not Ann." Mags seemed overly intent on dipping a fry into ketchup. "CJ and I might stray on the other side, but not our Ann. Nope."

"Uh, huh." Eric met my gaze. "I don't think you've told me everything."

"Mags, you have a big mouth."

"I can't help it if lying isn't my strong suit." Her eyes widened.

I explained about us searching Dickson's tent. "We didn't find anything, but Daniel and Rose overheard him telling someone he could get his hands on some money."

"Which means you intend to find out how." Eric exhaled heavily through his lips. "I'm glad you have Ann with you in case of trouble. The month is drawing to a close, CJ, and Robinson will be returning. What then?"

"We continue as usual. He won't tell us we can't wander the grounds." Unless someone complains.

"He won't, but I might." Eric leaned over and kissed me. "I know you won't stop, so please be careful. I won't be back tonight. I'm spending it in the woods. Someone is camping outside of designated areas. We don't want a forest fire."

Most definitely. With all the trees around us and no rain in a couple of weeks, a fire would be disastrous. "You be careful, too. You don't have anyone watching your back."

He tapped my nose with his forefinger. "I'm always careful." Another kiss, and he left on his green side-by-side, tossing a wave over his shoulder.

"I really need a man in my life," Mags said, watching him drive away. "I'm going to bake Robinson a cake when he gets back."

"You don't need a man to be fulfilled," Ann told her.

"I know that." Mags scowled. "But the company would be nice at night."

Ann shrugged. "I agree on that point."

"No boyfriend?" I asked.

"Not in a while. He decided he didn't want to be with a cop and skipped town." She stood and gathered up the garbage. "Some people can't take the worry, I guess. I don't mind being married to my job."

Liar. Being alone seemed to bother her more than she let on, if the stiff back and downturned mouth had anything to say. I wished I knew someone to introduce her to, but a prior isolated life left me with few friends outside my immediate circle.

"Let's make a plan for tonight," I said in an attempt to change the subject.

"We should wear black," Mags said. "We'll blend into the shadows better. I'll bring my Taser."

"Should I bring Caper?" I frowned. "I hate to leave her alone since someone is obviously trying to steal her, but she will bark. That's one thing for certain."

"Is there someone you can leave her with?" Ann

asked.

"Roy and Tammy, I guess." I glanced to where Caper nosed the ground for anything we might have dropped. "If you think she'll be safe."

"I say you muzzle her." Mags rolled her shoulders. "Even then, she'd be a warning of someone approaching."

"I don't own a muzzle." Besides, those things were awful. A dog should be allowed to be a dog. "I'll leave her with the Olsons."

"That's settled." Mags stood. "I'm going home to take a nap. It's going to be a long day." She hobbled away, getting quite good on her crutches.

"She can't go with us," Ann said. "Not on those. They're noisy and cumbersome. She might fall."

"How are you going to prevent her from coming?"

"I'll have to assert my authority and upset her." Ann followed Mags to her house.

I couldn't hear what was being said, but Mags's body language told me everything I needed to know. She was not a happy camper. The thing Ann didn't know was that no one told my friend what she could and couldn't do. If she didn't come with us, she'd go on her own, and that might be a whole lot more dangerous.

I turned and stared across the lake. Where are you, diamond thief? Why are you so concerned about my dog?

Chapter Sixteen

I wiled away the rest of the day cleaning my house, which didn't take long since it was under five-hundred square feet. Then I trimmed some bushes to fill up more time, did laundry, and sat outside with a glass of sweetened iced tea as a reward.

Ann had remained outside bent over a laptop, presumably because Davis had told her to do the background checks because he was too busy. That hadn't put her in a good mood. Another reason for me to have stayed inside and out of her way. She glanced up as if noticing me for the first time. "The three ladies are as clean as freshly bleached sheets." She put her head in her hands. "I'm completely lost. This whole case is over my head. I should rethink my career choice."

"No. I learned through the last mystery that it doesn't happen overnight. Instead, everything clicks all at once." When it does, you wonder why you didn't see it in the first place. At least that's how I felt. "Are we still heading over there after dark?"

She nodded. "Just don't get your hopes up about discovering anything."

"I'm going to drop Caper off."

Ann glanced in the direction I'd have to walk. "I guess you can go alone. I can see you all the way there. Go straight there and back."

"Yes, mom." The bodyguard thing was starting to get old. I wanted my house and my freedom back. I hooked a leash to Caper and set off for the Olsons' place.

Despite my yearning for solitude, I couldn't help but glance between each house, expecting someone to be lurking there. Last time, I'd simply stepped out my front door to take out the garbage and found myself at gunpoint. Not an experience I wanted to repeat.

I laughed and glanced at Caper. "I'm lying to myself. I actually find solving mysteries exciting. What about you?"

Caper gave a yip and wagged her tail. We were obviously of the same mind when it came to adventure.

Tammy got to feet from where she sat in front of her house. "The kids will love having a dog around even for a few hours."

"I appreciate you watching her. Keep her inside or on a leash. She tends to run off." I handed her the leash.

"We'll take good care of her. I'm sure she'll be spoiled when you come to get her." Tammy smiled and led my leaping dog into her house.

I know it was for the best since she liked to bark, but I couldn't help feeling a sense of betrayal at leaving her behind. Pretty much the same way I felt about Mags remaining at home.

"Psst."

I peered in the bushes to see Daniel gesturing at me. "What are you doing?"

"I feel a bit like a tattletale," he whispered, "but Mags told me y'all weren't taking her along. I saw her on a motorized scooter a few minutes ago headed for the campground. Can I come?"

Good grief. "No, you cannot. Stay here and protect my dog. Someone is out to get her. I'll take care of Mags." I really wished I had the confidence he'd stay behind, but that would make me naive. I gave him a stern look and hurried back to Ann. "Mags went across the lake."

She closed her eyes as if my words pained her. "Does she have a death wish?"

"You might think so." It wasn't even dark yet. Where did Mags plan on hiding? "What do you want to do?"

"We stick to the plan and go after dark when people are settling down." Her gaze drifted across the water. "Milton said he's off tonight and we're to call him if we need backup."

"Hopefully we won't encounter anyone." We were going to eavesdrop, not make an arrest.

We sat lost in our thoughts for the next hour as lanterns were lit and fires burned across the lake. Ann stood. "Let's go. Remember to use stealth. Follow my lead. If we're discovered, we're two friends out for an evening walk. You do realize I don't like bringing a civilian along on an investigation, right?"

"Got it." For that reason I chose not to dress in anything other than what I normally wore. Tee shirt and a pair of denim shorts. I wouldn't blend in with any shadows, but I'd be less suspicious if noticed. "Since you aren't supposed to leave me alone, you have no choice. When Milton was supposed to stay, and didn't, I was kidnapped and almost killed." Of course, I'd promised him I wouldn't leave my house. Who would have thought a killer would be hiding by my trashcan?

We took off at a jog, leaving the cart behind to further collaborate our story. By the time we arrived, I was winded. Ann didn't look as if she'd run anywhere. I really needed to start working out. "Give me a minute." I put a hand on her arm.

I bent over, balancing my hands on my knees, and struggled to breathe. After a few minutes, I straightened. "I'm good now." Not really, but I didn't feel as if I'd pass out.

Rather than follow the path, we stuck to the trees, moving from one cluster to another until we reached Dickson's site. Ann held a finger to her lips, and we hunkered down.

"I told you to trust me," he said into his cell phone. "They'll let down their guard, and I'll swoop in and grab the loot. We'll be set for life. Stop hounding me or I'll cut you out of the deal." He hung up and cursed, then grabbed a beer from the nearby cooler. "Fool. Doesn't know a good thing when it's right in front of him."

I glanced wide-eyed at Ann and mouthed, "the

diamonds."

She shook her head and moved away from the site. "We don't know for sure that he's talking about the diamonds. The man has been involved in get-rich schemes before. He's a con man and a swindler, so he could be talking about a scam."

My gut told me otherwise. "I guess, but I think he's talking about stealing the diamonds. If I had to guess further, I'd say from the three women. They may not have a police record, but that might just mean they've never been caught." I glimpsed Mags limping behind the tent at site 101. "Look."

Ann sighed. "Let's get her before she blows everything."

We darted forward and each took one of Mags's arms, dragging her into the bushes. "Where are your crutches?" I asked. "Do you want to permanently damage your knee?"

"I rented a scooter." She crossed her arms. "Since the two of you are so mean to not want me around, I decided to come myself." She wagged a finger in Ann's face. "I found something, too, but I don't think I'll tell you." She turned and started to limp away.

"Don't forget I'm a police officer and have the authority to arrest you," Ann called after her.

Mags stiffened. "Fine. Dickson plans on stealing something."

"We know that. We're trying to find out what and from whom." Ann rolled her eyes, the whites glowing in the moonlight. "Unless you have something more substantial to tell us, go home."

I could see the situation escalating like an

approaching storm. "Since she's already here, let her ride around the grounds on her scooter. She might see something." I glanced at Mags. "Stay on the scooter."

"Fine. You two have all the fun." She limped to where she'd parked the bright blue scooter behind the bathrooms, then climbed on and zipped away.

"I'll make it up to her later," Ann said. "I can't have her getting into trouble. On that bum knee, she'd be a rabbit hunkered in plain sight."

I understood. With Mags gone, Ann and I moved to a spot near site 101.

The three women sat in lawn chairs, glasses of wine in their hands, clearly celebrating something. I moved closer in an attempt to hear their conversation, skirting along the opposite side of the tent for coverage.

Ann grabbed my shirttail. "That's close enough," she whispered.

I nodded and stopped.

"I'm telling you I saw it plain as day," Myrna said. "Right out in the open."

"How do you plan on getting it? You can't very well snatch it in broad daylight." Ioda shook her head. "You should never have made the substitution in the first place."

"Lay off her," Carol said. "She did the best she could under the circumstances. It will all be worth it one day. Myrna will be the most sought-after leather goods maker around."

"That's the plan." Myrna raised her glass in a toast. "I'll come up with some way of getting what belongs to us."

"I hope it's better than the first plan." Ioda clinked her glass against her friends'.

Everything seemed to make sense, but without proof, we couldn't put the pieces together. Why couldn't someone come right out and say what they were doing instead of talking in riddles? What was in the open? What was substituted? I leaned against the tent.

The canvas sagged under me.

I gasped and clapped a hand over my mouth while trying not to fall.

"What was that?" Ioda jumped to her feet.

"A raccoon?" Carol suggested.

"No, bigger." Ioda started in our direction.

Mags sped by, honking her horn. The three women turned to face her. The diversion was all we needed. Ann and I sprinted away. Bless you, dear Mags.

"Crazy old bat!" Ioda yelled after our friend. "You're a menace to peaceful campers."

Mags caught up with us on the trail leading to the community. She stopped with a satisfied grin on her face. "See? You need me. You two were about to be caught. It's a good thing I happened by when I did."

"I'll admit it was a very good thing." Ann glared at me. "Clumsy here almost ruined everything."

"Sorry." I hitched my shoulders. "It's getting late, and I need to get my dog. Maybe if we sleep on what we heard today, it'll all make sense in the morning."

Ann moved aside to let Mags and her scooter lead the way. When we reached the Olson house,

Mags went home, and I fetched my pup.

"I can't figure out what it is they were talking about," Ann said as we strolled to my house. "What did she see?"

"I have—" I glanced down. The moonlight sparkled on the rhinestones glued to Caper's collar. I smiled. "The collar."

"What?" She frowned.

"What if they replaced the rhinestones on Caper's collar with diamonds? It's possible. They had put a plain leather collar on her until I got this one back." I'd nailed it—I just knew it.

"You might have something there." Ann scooped up Caper and dashed for the house. "I know who to call."

I raced after her, thankful we were almost home before breaking into a run. By the time we reached the front porch, Ann had Caper's collar off her neck.

I unlocked the front door and we rushed inside, locking it behind us. "Who are you calling?"

"The man who owned the jewelry store. He'll have what he needs to determine if these are real." She set Caper on the sofa and made the call. "He'll be here at eight in the morning." She held up her hand for a high-five. "Good job, CJ."

Feeling rather pleased with myself, I got a couple of glasses and filled them with ice and cold water. I handed one to Ann. "If Caper has been wearing the diamonds all this time, then Dickson also knows. That increases the amount of people wanting to get their hands on my poor puppy."

Ann smiled. "Looks like I'm bodyguard to both

of you."

"Not funny. I love this dog." I scowled. "I lost her once and it ripped my heart apart."

She put a hand on mine. "I won't let anything happen to your dog."

Something knocked against the outside wall. Ann motioned for me to be quiet, then plastered her back to the wall and peered out the curtains.

A rock flew through the window, shattering the glass.

Ann yelped and jumped back.

I screamed.

Caper barked.

Footsteps pounded away.

With my heart in my throat, I picked up the rock and read what had been written on it in black marker. "Give me the collar and no one gets hurt."

Chapter Seventeen

Davis showed up the next morning on the heels of the jewelry store owner. He stood with crossed arms and a stoic face while the man inspected Caper's collar.

A tired-looking Eric with two days of stubble on his handsome face wasn't far behind. "What did I miss?"

"We think Myrna Flutter substituted the rhinestones on the collar with diamonds," I said, handing him a cup of coffee.

"These are definitely the last of the stolen jewels." The man removed his eyepiece. "I guess we know who the thief is now."

A muscle ticked in Davis's jaw. "Ranger, want to escort me across the lake?"

Eric nodded. "Sure, but those three women skedaddled out of here at daybreak. I didn't know they were the ones responsible for the theft."

Davis looked ready to explode. "Those women

are virtual ghosts in our crime database. We can't find anything on them other than driver's license numbers. They each have different addresses. I'm willing to bet they won't be at any of them."

"What can we do?" Eric asked.

"Keep CJ and her dog out of trouble." The detective stalked to his car and drove off, the jewelry store owner with the collar right behind him.

Eric chuckled and glanced at me. "He isn't asking much, is he?"

"It's as if he doesn't know me at all," I said, grinning.

"Very funny." Ann stood from the picnic table. "With those women gone, there will be a whole lot of sitting around doing nothing until they're caught. That's the most boring thing I've ever heard of."

"I still have to do my rounds. If I learned anything at all with the last round of thefts, it's that the person responsible will be back." I shuddered.

"Maybe you should take a vacation," Eric suggested. "If you aren't here, they won't be able to find you."

"Tempting, but Robinson isn't back yet. I can't let him down." I cupped my hands around my mostly undrunk coffee. With it being my second cup that morning, and the heat index rising, I considered switching to iced coffee. Anything to keep my mind from dwelling on the fact that some dangerous people had gotten away.

"You need some fun." Eric sat next to me. "Have you given more thought to Mags's suggestion of a barbeque?"

"No." What a good idea. It might draw those women out of their hiding place and result in their capture. Especially if I appeared unconcerned enough to throw a get-together. "Let's plan it for next weekend. Will you man the grill again?"

"You bet. In fact, I'll spring for the burgers and hot dogs."

"See, Ann? We need to go to town. Something to do." I grinned and headed for the house.

Inside, I retrieved Caper and slipped the leather collar Myrna had put on her, then locked up the house with the dog inside. Since she no longer wore a lot of money around her furry neck, no one would need to steal her.

To save time, we stopped first at an office supply store to design and print off the fliers. The shindig would be a potluck for side dishes and desserts. My stomach already rumbled in anticipation of good ole Southern food. With each task we marked off my virtual list, my spirits lifted.

Not so with Ann. Her frown deepened with each passing hour.

"What's wrong?" I asked.

"I wanted to be the one to catch the diamond thief. It would've been wonderful for my career."

"Stop being such a baby. You might still be the one. I told you they'd be back."

"Why?" She raised her eyebrows. "You don't have the collar anymore."

"They don't know that. I seriously doubt they stuck around to see Davis and the jeweler at my house."

She perked up. "That's right. They'll be back to

take the collar by force, and I'll clap the cuffs on them."

Ann seemed overly excited at my impending danger. "Great." I parked in front of the one-and-only grocery store in our small town. "Let's split up and divide the shopping." I handed her the list for drinks and buns while I kept my personal shopping and what I'd need to bring for a side dish. Texas taco salad. Yum.

Ann headed for the bread aisle and I headed for the chips. I tossed two bags of Doritos in my cart, then turned the corner to locate the French dressing before heading to produce. I'd no sooner wrapped my fingers around a bottle when I heard a voice I recognized and froze.

"I'm going to personally wring her neck," Myrna said. "No one else touch her."

"Can't we take turns?" Ioda asked.

"You two talked me into committing a crime and we got nothing out of it." Something thunked into a cart. Carol griped, "You killed a man, Myrna."

Darn it. A confession of sorts and I'd have no way of proving it. I sent a quick text to Ann letting her know the women were in aisle ten.

Stall them.

How?

Any way you can.

My phone rang out "Chitty Chitty Bang Bang." Oh no.

Three angry faces rounded the corner and blocked my escape.

"Hello, ladies. What can I do for you?" I forced

a smile.

"Shut up and come with us," Myrna said, baring her teeth.

A commotion to her right sent all three of them running as Ann yelled out. "Stop, police." So much for our pretense of being friends. Ann gave chase after the women, who'd barged through the swinging doors at the end of the store. I left my cart and sprinted after them.

I skidded to a halt amongst boxes of dried foods. Spotting a door to my right, I headed out into the afternoon sun, blinking against the sudden harsh glare. A few yards away, I caught a glimpse of Ann still giving chase and shouting into her cell phone.

Why is there always running with her? I groaned and kept following. The last thing I wanted was for those women to circle around and find me too far away from Ann.

I rounded the corner and stopped on the street next to Ann. "Where are they?"

"They hopped in a waiting car and sped off. Green Sonata, no license plate." She gave the description to whoever was on the other end of the line.

"We might as well retrieve our groceries," I said, heading back to the store. "I told you they'd be back, and they will again." Unfortunately. I put a hand to my heaving chest, almost wishing for a motorized cart.

"You need to get in better shape," Ann said. "You're young, you're thin, and can't run a mile."

"I could if something was chasing me." I grinned and held the store door open for her. "Like a bear…or a zombie. That would get me going."

She rolled her eyes and laughed. "Sorry I blew my cover, but I couldn't let them take you."

"I'm glad of that." Still, I'd need to be away from the community and campgrounds more in case we spotted them again. Maybe I'd have Ann remain close but out of sight in order to entice Myrna and the others to come after me. I hated being bait, but it did seem to be the most effective way to catch the crooks.

We paid for our purchases and headed home to hang up fliers on both the tiny house-community board and the campground. The barbeque was almost a week away, which gave people enough time to participate. The larger the crowd, the better those evil women could blend in.

I stored the non-perishable food in my loft and stared into my refrigerator in a vain attempt to put away the other purchased items. I had room for a full-size fridge. It could be time to purchase one and stop putting square food in round holes.

"Are you trying to cool down Arkansas?" Ann plopped onto the sofa.

"I don't have enough space."

"Of course not. It's a tiny house. Call Mags. She might have room in her fridge."

I did, and she did, so Ann and I carried what wouldn't fit in mine to Mags's. "It's mainly ice cream," I said. "I almost bought tomatoes and lettuce for the salad I'm taking, but realized it was too early."

"You should have asked me to go." She shoved the food into her fridge. "I needed a few things. You know I can't drive yet."

"Doesn't Tammy do your shopping for you?"

"Yes, but I still like getting out of the house."

"I'm sorry. I'll remember next time. It isn't as if you could have run with us." Uh oh.

"Why were you running?" She tilted her head.

"Uh, we saw Myrna and the others."

"So? You're keeping secrets, CJ." She tapped me in the chest.

I explained about the dog collar and the dash from the grocery store. "None of which was planned."

She looked deep in thought. "We don't have an address to check out?"

"Davis is taking care of that," Ann said. "Did you notice the items in their cart?"

My eyes widened. "It was the type of stuff you take camping. There isn't another campground within miles."

"My guess," Mags said, "is that they're heading into the woods. What better place to hide than acres and acres of thick forest? You might want to let Eric know what we're thinking. He can keep his eyes open. I'm getting around much better now. Anyone interested in a hike?"

"No," Ann and I said in unison.

"If they aren't captured by the barbeque, and you have a doctor's order saying it's okay, then we can go." Ann narrowed her eyes. "I mean it, Mags. If you go it alone, I'll arrest you."

"I'm not brave enough to venture into the wilderness alone." She shook her head as if Ann's head was as hard as petrified wood. "I can't hike with crutches either. I'm already getting callouses on my hands. What do you take me for?"

"A stubborn old woman."

"You can come with me to put up fliers," I suggested. "It isn't town, but it's out of the house."

"Sure. We might see something important." She grabbed her crutch and headed out the front door.

I turned to Ann. "Why do you antagonize her?"

"She needs to see the importance of doing what I tell her. Especially in her condition."

True, but Mags needed handling with gentle hands, not barked orders. "Find a more subtle way."

"I'll try, but I've always been rather blunt."

We joined Mags in the golf cart. I spotted Daniel with a backpack and sleeping bag on his back and blocked the road. "Where are you going?"

"Camping. Dad said I could."

"There might be bad people out there."

"Might being the magic word. It's summer, CJ. I can't stay cooped up in the house all day. I want to find a creek, catch my own food, and have some peace and quiet." He hitched the pack more firmly on his shoulders. "I'm only going to be gone two nights and three days." He marched off whistling.

"Nothing we can do if his parents gave permission," Ann said. "He seems like a smart boy. He'll be alright. Myrna and the others have no reason to mess with him. All the diamonds and jewelry have been accounted for."

"Losing a life of wealth made three women angry." I thought of them wanting to take turns strangling me.

"Everyone knows angry women are dangerous,"

Mags pointed out. "We'd be much better off if it was a man after us. A psycho female is like a rabid skunk. Ask any man."

Now, there's a picture.

Chapter Eighteen

Not a peep or a sight from any of the former residents of site 101 the whole next week. In fact, we'd filled their empty campsite within two days with a lovely family of five.

Robinson had returned, thus eliminating half my workload. I dove into plans for the barbeque with the full intention of catching three mean crooks and then getting back to my peaceful, often boring life, which I've decided I preferred.

I loaded my enormous Texas taco salad and all the paper products into the back of my cart, barely leaving room for Ann. She sat perched on one hip and hung on for her life as we went to pick up Mags.

She glanced at the full cart. "Guess I'm holding my possum pie on my lap."

"Possum pie?" I grinned. "I love that."

Ann grimaced. "Why in the world would anyone eat possum?"

"It doesn't have that critter in it." Mags rolled her eyes. "It's a chocolate pie in layman's terms."

"Thank God." Ann relaxed, but yelped and grabbed the seat when we lurched forward. "Be careful or everything back here is going to be on the ground, including me."

I lifted a hand in apology and continued to speed toward the opposite side of the lake. Roy had erected a few canopies to provide shade near the lake's edge, and already people were dragging lawn chairs to claim their spot. It promised to be a good turnout. Hopefully enough people for Myrna and her cohorts to sneak into the crowd.

"Too many people," Ann said when I stopped the cart and she jumped out, holding things in place to keep them from tumbling to the grass. "Don't leave my side, CJ."

I didn't plan on it, but spotting Eric near a grill, I immediately grabbed an armload of paper plates and set off toward him.

"CJ." Ann hurried to my side. "Do you ever listen?"

"I heard you. If wouldn't take but a moment for you to run to my rescue when I'm only a few yards away. Look, Davis and Milton are here, too." I pointed to where the men stood chatting with Amber. They must think our evil threesome would show up same as I did.

"Wait for me," Mags called. "I can't run on crutches."

I slowed, tossing her a smile. "Sorry. I'm just

excited to see Eric. I haven't gotten to spend much time with him the last few weeks."

"Well, he ain't going anywhere today." She huffed and hobbled along between me and Ann. "Don't worry, Ann. I won't let her disappear."

Great. They'd both be stuck to my rear like a pair of ticks. I'd be lucky to catch a glimpse of Myrna.

We set the supplies on a table under one of the canopies before I finally got a greeting kiss from Eric. "I miss you."

He smiled. "I miss you more."

"Not possible." I gave him another kiss, then stood back to survey the crowd.

Teenagers had started a game of soccer. Younger children played chase under the watchful eyes of their parents. Men and women clustered together, filling the air with chatter and laughter. If we made get-togethers a regular occurrence, we'd always keep Heavenly Acres and the campground full.

"You look quite pleased with yourself," Milton said.

"I am."

"Why don't you go into law enforcement and save us all the headache of having to save your skinny rear end?" His lips twitched. "You're giving Davis gray hair."

"Ha. I cannot help it if I seem to attract trouble or that I have an insatiable curiosity."

"You know what they say about curiosity killing the cat." He clapped me on the shoulder and sauntered away.

Milton and I got along better since he'd had to be my bodyguard a little while back, something I'd caused him to fail at, but our personalities still clashed. Too bad. He could be the father I never had since mine died when I was young. Milton thought me a young fool, and I thought him a grumpy old man.

"He really does like you," Eric said, his lips close to my ear, tickling the tiny hairs there. "He wouldn't rag on you so much if he didn't."

I smiled. "I kind of like him, too, but he is irritating."

He laughed. "No argument there." He returned to the grill and I kept watching the crowd, knowing it was doubtful Myrna or one of the others would show their faces with three police officers and a park ranger in attendance. Still I searched the crowd like a falcon looking for a field mouse.

"Relax." Mags thumped next to me. "You look like a feral cat."

I shrugged. "I was thinking something noble like a falcon."

"Either way, you aren't very subtle." She handed me a plastic cup of lemonade. "If they come, they'll snatch you when you go to the bathroom."

I cut her a quick glance. "Thanks."

"Or, they might have decided flight was the better option than revenge and you are perfectly safe." She patted my arm. "Don't worry, dear. Ann or I will go with you. Is that Ioda?" She pointed toward a woman jogging along the lake. "No, it isn't. Too bad."

"I've never met someone as thirsty for adventure as myself."

She grinned. "The difference is I'm braver than you. You like the thrill, but you're also a scaredy-cat."

True. "I'm always at odds with myself."

"Never boring."

"Exciting to be around."

"A bit conceited."

"What?" I narrowed my eyes. "I thought we were playing 'Then You Zing Me with an Insult.'"

"You don't agree?" Her eyes widened.

"No. I'm the least selfish person I know."

"You don't know many people, dear."

"I don't want to do this anymore. You're mean." I raised the cup to my lips to stop their trembling. She'd hurt my feelings and actually meant the words she said.

"Eric, come soothe this girl's ruffled feathers, I've scouting to do." Mags thumped away.

I waved a hand to tell him I was fine. A flock of young women vied for his attention anyway. I doubted many of them ate much of anything, but they all wanted a hot dog that day. I decided to mosey Amber's way to pick her brain after Davis left her side. Surely Davis let something spill during their "pillow" talk.

"He's been particularly tight-lipped," she said when I asked, "but I did gather that there is a diamond ring still missing."

"If they hid it around here, then they won't have gone far. It's all they have left." I clapped my hands. Caper's daily walks would increase. With her ability to find shiny objects, she might be what we needed to capture the three women.

"What are you cooking up now?" Amber crossed her arms and glanced at Davis, who watched us with a stern expression. "I can't help you. I like him and don't want to jeopardize our relationship."

"You won't have to. Caper will be all I need." I'd let her off her leash and follow wherever she went.

"Please don't take my grandmother with you."

"Mags is more determined than I am. Don't worry. Ann follows me wherever I go. She even waits outside the door when I take a shower, like anyone can get to me in my tiny house. She could be anywhere and block their entrance."

She laughed. "Davis said she takes her job very seriously, and when she stops bending rules for her friends, she'll be a good police officer."

It warmed me to know Ann considered me not just a job, but a friend. "She'll be good because she takes risks. Sticking too close to the book is what lets crooks get away."

"You'll never convince my handsome detective of that."

"I don't guess I could." I took another sip of the tart drink in my hand. I really did need to use the restroom and was sorely tempted to go alone. Only the thought of Ann getting in trouble if something happened to me sent me to where she stood on a slight hill in order to watch the proceedings better. "I need to visit the little girl's room."

"Thank you for coming to get me."

Together we climbed the rest of the hill and went into the brick building housing the shower and toilet stalls. Ann stood between the toilets and the door as I closed the stall. I heard her run someone off, telling them to wait five more minutes. I shook my head and did my business.

As I turned to press the handle to flush with my foot, I noticed a hole in the wall behind the tank. Not unusual in a place this old, but I'd checked this building thoroughly for needed repairs on my first day. If someone had vandalized the wall, I'd hunt them down and make them fix it themselves.

I picked up a piece of plaster from the floor and started to insert it into the hole. Something sparkled up at me. I stuck my fingers inside, praying there weren't any spiders. I hated spiders. I withdrew my hand and smiled down at a gorgeous diamond ring.

"Are you almost finished?" Ann asked. "There's a child who needs to use the restroom."

"No need to keep a child out." I rolled my eyes and slipped the ring into my pocket. These rooms were kept unlocked. Why would the ring still be here?

I flushed and joined Ann. "Ready to head back." I flashed a grin and held the door open for a scowling mother and a dancing child. "Sorry. My friend is a bit zealous."

"Careful," Ann said. "I'm careful."

When we returned to the barbeque, I pulled Mags aside on the pretense of watching the sun kiss the surface of the lake. "I found the missing diamond ring."

"What ring?"

I explained what Amber had told me. "The question I have is…if the women put it there, why haven't they retrieved it? It would be a simple thing to do during the night hours."

She tapped her finger against her lips. "That's a good question. If I were a thief, why would I put something somewhere and not retrieve it right away, unless—" She grinned. "What if one of the three is pulling the wool over the eyes of the other two?"

"As in hiding it away to keep it for themselves? Mags, you're brilliant." I gave her a quick hug. "If your theory is right, then it hasn't been retrieved because the one person hasn't been able to get away from the other two."

"What do we do with this information?"

I shrugged. "I'm debating whether or not to turn the ring over to Davis. I'd like to draw the thief into the open."

"The person will be frantic when they discover the ring gone. That alone will draw them out. You need to turn it in. We can catch the culprit without them actually hunting you down for their stolen property."

"True, they don't yet know that it's me who found the ring." I hurried over to Davis and pulled the ring from my pocket. "Interested?"

His lips stretched into a smile. "You aren't the one I thought would present me with an engagement ring, but I'll accept." He held out his hand.

I dropped the ring into his palm and explained where I'd found it and Mags's theory. "Makes sense."

"Yes, it does." He stared up the hill toward the brick building. "So which woman is the traitor and how do we get her to come out of hiding?"

Chapter Nineteen

"The best idea I can come up with is to spread the news that I found a ring in the women's restroom. No one needs to know I gave it to you."

"Use you as bait, you mean." He clenched his jaw.

"Sort of, but with Ann always by my side, I should be safe enough." I doubted the traitor would bring her friends along to retrieve what she'd taken from the group. Ann and I could definitely handle one woman. Okay, Ann could. She had the gun. I'd step out long enough to lure out the culprit, then step back and let Ann handle things.

"I can see you wrestling with what you will or will not do from here." Davis dropped the ring into the front pocket of his shirt. "Unfortunately, I agree with your idea. Tell Mags about the ring and tell her to act as if she's giving away a secret or something."

I nodded and hurried back to my friend to let her

know about our scheme. "Will you do it?"

"You bet." She rubbed her hands together. "In fact, you can come along and act irritated with me for blabbing. That shouldn't be hard."

Wouldn't be hard at all. Especially after her previous comments about me being conceited. That description didn't fit me at all. I didn't wear designer clothes and rarely wore makeup.

"Stop pouting." Mags clunked toward a group of campers in lawn chairs next to the water. Rather than talk to them, she turned to me and spoke in a loud whisper that anyone in the near vicinity could hear.

"I cannot believe your luck." Mags wiggled her eyebrows. "Finding that diamond ring in the women's restroom. What now?"

"I, uh, wait to see if anyone claims it." A good idea, actually. I'd post a notice on the bulletin board. If the women were snooping around, they were bound to see it.

"It's got to be worth a lot of money. You could sell it."

"Great idea." We turned and headed for the next group of people and repeated the process. Within an hour, everyone in attendance was buzzing about the ring I'd found. Grinning, I tore off a section of a paper tablecloth and scribbled a "Lost and Found" note. Then, with Ann by my side, I headed to the camp bulletin board and tacked it up.

"I'm glad the two of you didn't describe the ring," Ann said. "There will be a lot of liars calling the hotline. Only someone with a real connection will know the truth."

"I'm exhausted over the whole thing." We took the long way back to the barbeque, scanning the trees for any sign of Myrna and her friends. The hotline was actually a burner phone Ann handed me that took calls from my phone to it. I'd be taking the calls, but every conversation would be recorded and sent to Davis. We'd covered all our bases, I hoped. My regular phone would ring out its normal melody in case the crook was close enough to hear.

By five o'clock, the gathering started breaking up as kids whined for lack of a nap, mothers had creases in their foreheads from keeping their children from wandering off, and most people sported a sunburn. It had been a successful day at getting people to converse and maybe make new friends.

"What's this?" I turned to see Robinson, a puzzled expression on his face.

"A barbeque," I said. "Very well attended."

"I can't compete with this." He frowned.

"You won't have to. I'll always include the campgrounds in any gathering we throw for Heavenly Acres." I handed him a black garbage bag full of trash. "Do you mind? If you're hungry, Eric has some burgers left over."

"I could eat." He shook his head and headed for the grill, a bag slung over his back like a grumpy Santa.

I sighed. Not once had I considered he wouldn't like the fact I'd thrown a barbeque. The man seemed content to patrol the grounds once a day and sit in front of his trailer the rest of the time, watching the world go by. Maybe it would be a good thing for Mags to set her cap for him. She'd definitely get him involved in living again…if he'd let her.

Eric stared impassively at the older man as Robinson ranted. Then he handed him a burger and bun and clapped a hand on his shoulder.

I approached when Robinson tossed the trash in a dumpster and strode off to his trailer. "I had no idea he'd react this way."

"Don't take it personal." Eric closed the lid to the grill. "Turns out it wasn't much of a vacation. Robinson headed to his childhood home to finalize a sale. He'll feel better about it all tomorrow."

I glanced in the direction he'd gone, my heart aching for his loss. "I can relate." Of course, I hadn't listed Grams' house yet. Someday, when I was ready to start a family, the one-hundred-year-old house with a wraparound porch might be the very place I'd want to live.

"Let's finish up here and go home. The others might have enjoyed a day watching the water, but you and I have been working." Eric wrapped an arm around my waist and pulled me in for a kiss. "I also think you, Davis, and Mags have cooked something up. I'd like to be privy to the information."

Once we'd cleaned up and drove back to my house, I told him about what had happened that afternoon. Ann and Mags remained silent in the rear of the cart and let me do the talking. I finished just as Eric parked in front of my house.

He turned to face me. "I cannot believe Davis went along with this. It's too dangerous."

"Not really. Ann is here." I smiled. "No one can

get to me without going through her."

"Not even Ann can stop an unexpected bullet, CJ."

Ann hopped from the back. "That's why I wear a Kevlar vest." She thumped her chest. "Didn't know that, did you?"

I laughed. "No, but I'm glad of it." I scooped a groggy Caper into my arms. Child after child had run the banks of the lake with one end of her leash in hand. My dog was officially worn out, and I hadn't had to worry about her.

"I'll make coffee," I said, heading into the house. I set Caper on her bed next to the sofa and stepped into my tiny galley-style kitchen. As I popped a pod into the Keurig, I stared at the brick building across the lake. It was fortunate indeed that I'd come across the ring and not someone else. This way, it had been turned over to the authorities with the thief none the wiser. If someone other than me or the suspects had found the ring, we wouldn't have known it existed.

"What are you thinking about?" Eric leaned in the doorway.

"How things just happen." I removed the cup and added another. "When I took this job, I thought it the perfect time to chill after so many years as a caregiver. Thievery, murder, debauchery…it hasn't ended since my first day." I locked gazes with him. "I don't believe in coincidences. This has all happened for a reason."

"What do you think that reason is?" He accepted the cup I offered him.

"Confidence, strength, all the things I didn't

think I had?" I shrugged. "I call myself a big chicken, but when the hammer comes down, I've faced death in the face not once, but twice." Grams would either be scandalized or proud.

"You're enjoying yourself for the first time in years is what it sounds like to me."

"Is that bad?"

He smiled. "No, I only wish you'd found another way to gain confidence."

"Sorry." My smile widened.

"No, you aren't." He took the other cup from me. "I'll give this to Ann. You can bring out yours and Mags's." He tossed me a wink, then strolled out the door.

A few minutes later, I stepped outside with two mugs and saw I needed two more. Amber and Davis had joined the impromptu party. Pooh. I'd wanted some time alone with Eric. I set the coffee on the table and headed inside to make two more cups.

They were deep in a conversation about how to keep me safe when I handed out the last of the cups. The phone in my pocket rang out "Chitty Chitty Bang Bang." I pulled it out. "Hello?"

"Give me the ring or I'll kill you and your little dog, too," an electronic voice said.

"It's the wicked witch from *The Wizard of Oz*," I told the others. "She wants the ring."

"Stop playing around. You'll see how serious the situation is when we come face-to-face."

"I can't wait." I smiled at the others staring at me. "Bye now." I hung up. "I don't think that was a prank call."

"Could you tell who it was?" Davis asked.

"Disguised their voice, but it was definitely a woman."

"Which we already know." He stared into his coffee. "Did she tell you where to take the ring?"

I shook my head. "I'm sure she'll call again."

His phone dinged. "There's the recording of the conversation. I'll have the lab run it through some tests and see if we can pick up anything that will tell us who the caller is." He gave Amber a tender kiss on the cheek, warned her about giving me anymore slipped information, then climbed into his car and drove away.

Mags's eyes twinkled. "Things are getting serious with you two."

Amber blushed. "Maybe. I really do like him."

"I seem to be the only one alone." She glanced across the lake. "I think I'll take Robinson a casserole tomorrow."

I still couldn't see what she saw in the man, but to each their own. "I'm sure it will be appreciated. The next time I get a call, I'm going to set up a meeting."

Ann exhaled sharply through her nose. "Be wise when you do. Make it a public place where I can blend in without being seen."

"I'll do my best, but I might not have much choice. Maybe you could wire me?" It worked in my favorite crime shows.

As if she could read my mind, Ann said, "This isn't television."

"It might still work," Mags said. "Look at all that hair of CJ's. You could hide anything in there."

I groaned. That meant wearing my hair down. I

grew hot and sweaty just thinking about it. "That's a good idea, actually." With my tiny frame, I didn't have many places on my body to hide anything.

Ann folded her hands on the table in front of her. "Listen closely. When the call comes, you do your best to set the time and the place. When you go, you'll tell us everything around you, people, places, directions....fit it into the conversation somehow."

"I'd like to set it up for the chapel."

"Why?" Her brow furrowed.

"The walls are mostly windows. You'll be able to see everything you can't hear."

"That's actually an excellent idea," Eric said.

"I know." Hope filled me. "What's a safer place than a church?"

Ann nodded. "We can always shoot the suspect if things start going in the wrong direction."

"No, we just had the windows replaced. You will not shatter them with a bullet."

"Not even if it means your life?"

"Not even then." I scowled. "I'll think of somewhere else to meet."

She shook her head. "The chapel is the best idea you've had, and the foliage outside is thick enough for not only me to hide, but Milton and Davis." She grinned for the first time in hours. "Let's catch a crook."

My phone rang.

Chapter Twenty

The phone rang only once. I raised a quizzical brow. "Wrong number?"

Ann shrugged. "Or they're toying with you. Let's go to bed. You don't want to be lacking sleep when you come face-to-face with this person."

True. Still, I tossed and turned on the mattress in my loft. Every sound outside had me crawling to the tiny window above my head. Silly, really. No one could get to me with Ann sleeping at the foot of the stairs. I'd finally fallen asleep when the phone rang.

"Just want you to know that while you sleep, I'm plotting." Click.

"Was that her?" Ann called from below.

"Yep. Just telling me she's plotting against me." I let my arms fall back against the mattress. If I were honest with myself, and it was time I was, I enjoyed being the hunter, not the prey. Yet, I never found the culprit until they stalked me. There had to be a better way to get my mystery fix without putting myself in danger.

I fell asleep to the electronic voice telling me to run. I'd glance over my shoulder to see a faceless woman with a gun pointed at me. I woke to the sound of a gunshot.

"What is it?" I bolted to a sitting position.

"Sorry. I dropped a pan," Ann said. "I thought I'd cook us some eggs and bacon."

I put a hand over my racing heart and lay back down. What a way to wake up. The dream had seemed so real. Dressed in black with no distinguishing features, the woman in the dream could have been Carol, Ioda, or Myrna.

Over coffee, eggs, bacon, and toast, I explained the dream to Ann. "I'm sure it's because I got the call right before going to sleep. No one can tell the future, right? Not a lot of chance she's going to chase me through the woods." *Please say that won't happen.*

"I believe in premonition," she said, not alleviating my fears. "Look around you. You're surrounded by forest. The likelihood of being chased at gunpoint isn't too far-fetched." She grinned. "Don't worry. They'll have to go through me first."

"You aren't immortal," I mumbled, popping a piece of bacon into my mouth. Why did I rate having a 24/7 police protector? Other people found themselves in danger once in a while. I glanced down at Caper. But how many of them had their poor puppy stuck in a canoe and set afloat? I had to see this through.

My phone rang. The number on the screen

showed Eric. "Good morning."

"Good morning to you," he said. "Don't hold breakfast for me."

"We've already eaten."

"Good. I've got a report of smoke near the abandoned ranger station and need to check it out. I'll see you tonight, hopefully."

"Tonight." I smiled as he hung up and Kim Rowe approached.

"Here are your fragrances." She handed us each a white paper sack. "Thank you for your purchase." She forced a smile and went back the way she'd come.

Feeling like a child at Christmas, I pulled out a bottle of perfume uniquely mine. I popped the top and spritzed my neck, breathing deeply. Flowers and a hint of something darker. "I love it."

"Mine's gardenia." Ann sprayed her neck before setting the bottle on the table. She sniffed. "Do you smell smoke?"

I raised my nose. "I do." I stood and glanced down the road. "One of the trashcans—"

A gunshot shattered Ann's perfume.

She jumped up and tackled me to the ground. "Be still." She pulled her weapon from the holster on her hip. "The fire was a diversion."

"We still have to put it out. It's right next to a house." I struggled from underneath her and, keeping low, grabbed a bucket, filled it with water, and rushed to the fire with Ann on my heels. I dumped the contents of the bucket on the fire, dousing the flames.

"That makes me so mad." Ann glowered. "That

perfume was expensive." She took my arm and dragged me back to the house. "Get inside."

"I need to get Caper first." I turned. "Where is she?" The leash attached to the lead rope was lying empty on the ground. "Caper?" I looked under the house. "She used the fire to steal my dog." For the first time since my cousin died in a drive-by shooting years ago, I wanted a gun in my hand. "Why take my dog?" I whirled and glared at Ann.

"Leverage. She's probably—"

My phone rang and I grabbed it from my pocket. "Where's my dog?"

"Sitting comfortably in a cage. The ring for the dog."

"Meet me at the chapel tonight."

"I don't think so." She chuckled. "I'm calling the shots. It will have to be at a time and place I designate."

"You mean after the other two women are asleep? Which one are you?"

"The smart one." Click.

"What did she say?" Ann ushered me into the house.

I snagged my perfume on the way.

"That she'll set the time and place." I plopped onto the sofa. Caper hadn't been hurt the last time she'd been taken. Hopefully, this time wouldn't be any different.

A knock on the door had Ann answering with gun in hand. "Oh, it's just Mags." She stepped back and let the other woman enter.

"I heard a gunshot, and it smells like smoke and flowers outside." She crossed her arms and glanced from Ann to me. "What did I miss?"

I let Ann explain it to her. My mind was too busy trying to figure out where I'd be summoned to exchange a ring I didn't have for my pup.

After Ann explained the morning's events to Mags, she stepped away to call Davis. Away wasn't far when your house was under five-hundred square feet. Even with her lowering her voice, I could hear her telling him she wanted to spirit me away someplace safer.

"Absolutely not," I said. "I need to be close by. What if she wants me to meet her at a moment's notice?"

She narrowed her eyes. "Davis said to shelter in place and to let him know when a meeting is scheduled."

"That's the best plan, considering no one can take CJ's place." Mags propped her crutches against the wall and sat next to me. "The thief has seen her, talked with her. What about Dickson? Have you questioned him?"

"Milton said he went by his campsite yesterday and he had packed up and gone." Ann paced—well, took three steps in one direction, then turned and took three back. "The same day as the women."

"In cahoots?" I asked.

"We don't think so. We think he merely moved on because they did."

Made sense. He'd overheard them talking and left when his chance to get rich had disappeared. It didn't matter. We had only three suspects now.

"I bet Ioda is the traitor." Mags nodded a few times. "She's the bossy one. Carol is quiet and

Myrna is a peace-loving hippie type."

"My bet is Myrna," I said. "She's the one who had Caper before and most likely made the leather collar and switched them out. Of course, in the movies, it's often the quiet one."

"We'll find out soon enough," Ann said. "If she stops playing games and calls you. I hate waiting around."

"Stop pacing before you make me dizzy." Mags stuck out her foot to prevent Ann from taking any more steps. "Use your time to figure out how to keep our girl safe."

"I am keeping her safe." Ann frowned.

"So safe that a bullet was fired at your perfume bottle with both of you sitting there at leisure. That bullet could have easily gotten you or CJ. You can't prevent long-distance attacks. What if the bottle wasn't the target?" She raised her eyebrows.

I shuddered. "I don't think I was, but I did feel the rush of air as it zipped past me. I think Ann was the target, and the shooter missed."

Ann sagged into the only chair in my house. "I've never been shot at before."

"Get used to it." Mags laughed. "This sort of thing seems to happen around CJ."

"Ha ha." I rested my head against the sofa back. I didn't like waiting either and guessed that the caller would enjoy making me sweat. "I'm not sure we'll hear any time soon."

"Why don't you go order another bottle of perfume?" Mags asked.

"I can do that over the phone." Ann called Kim Rowe and placed the order. "Thank goodness she keeps her recipes. I hate having to pay that amount of money again."

Boredom set in within the hour. I flipped through television channels and settled on a true-crime documentary about cold cases. Even that failed to keep my interest for long. Ann and Mags were no better. Mags had taken to thumping her crutch on the wooden floor and Ann back to walking to and fro.

"You two are driving me nuts. I need to make my rounds." I started to get up.

Ann waved me back down. "You aren't going anywhere. Roy can handle things."

I groaned and settled back down. "It's my job to make sure my tenants are happy."

"They'll survive a day without you." Her cop face slipped into place.

I gave a heavy sigh and turned back to the television. I halfway watched, my mind still analyzing last night's dream, when the picture of a young woman flashed on the screen. "That's Carol." Except her name was Mae Johnson. "Look. She's the main suspect in the twenty-year disappearance of a little girl."

Ann moved to where she could see. "Stole the daughter she'd lost custody of two days after being released from prison for armed robbery." Her face lit up. "We know who the traitor is. No wonder we couldn't find any background on her. The department thought she'd simply stayed out of trouble." She called Davis, turning back to me when she hung up. "This will cement my career if I can solve this cold case."

"What do you think happened to the child?" I asked. "The narrator said she needed medication for diabetes."

Ann shrugged. "Hopefully, Mae took care of her, and the child is grown up and happy. As for our diamond thief, I'm sure Carol/Mae, Ioda, and Myrna all played a part."

"Mae's the ringleader." Mags smirked. "CJ was right. The quiet one is always the one to watch."

I didn't feel a sense of accomplishment over a lucky guess. "Let's save the rejoicing until she's in handcuffs and I'm still breathing."

"Good idea." She patted my arm. "I kind of like having you around."

A nervous laugh escaped me. "That makes two of us."

At the sound of a car pulling up front, Ann peered out the curtains. "A delivery van is carrying a box toward the house. Now he's setting it on the porch." A knock sounded. Ann waved for us to stay put. "Now he's leaving."

"Open the door and get the box, Miss Paranoid," Mags said.

"What if it's a bomb?" My eyes widened.

"She isn't going to blow you up until she has the ring."

"Good point." Ann opened the door and retrieved a small, square box. She set it on the coffee table. "Who wants the honors?"

"It's addressed to me, so I will." I took a deep breath and cut the tape holding the top on. I slowly lifted off the lid and set it aside. I gasped. Staring up at me, duct tape over his mouth, was Eric tied to a chair in what looked like a cave. Even in the photo, the look in his eyes could kill. In a cage next to him lay Caper.

My phone rang. I grabbed it from where I'd set it on the sofa next to me. "Hello, Mae."

"Aren't you the clever girl? I see you received my package."

"I did." She had to be close in order to see the delivery. I peered out the window. "What now?"

"Meet me at the boat dock tonight at ten o'clock. Come alone or both these cuties die."

Chapter Twenty-one

"Stick this to your, uh…" Davis waved a wire in front of my chest.

"My bra? What? A big guy like you can't mention women's underwear in mixed company?" I turned around and clipped it to my bra strap. All joking aside, fear ripped through me at the thought I might fail Caper and Eric. Wired for sound, I turned around. "I'm ready. Are you?" My voice shook.

"We won't let anything happen to you," Ann said, placing a hand on my shoulder. "I'll be close by."

"Not too close. She can't see you."

"We had a duplicate made. Try stalling as long as possible before giving it to her." Davis dropped a fake diamond ring into my hand.

It did look real. I took a deep breath, slipped the ring into the left pocket of my jean shorts, and glanced at the clock. I had fifteen minutes to get to the dock. Without another word, I ran out of my house and sprinted for the meeting place.

The night was something out of a horror flick. Storm clouds blocked the moon and stars. A wind blew, rubbing tree leaves together with sinister whispers. I couldn't let my imagination run away with me. What were the chances of running through the rain and almost dying in the mud for the second time? I glanced at the clouds. Please, don't rain.

While I didn't expect my meeting with Mae to be easy, I didn't expect to wait for half an hour either. "I don't see her," I whispered into my chest.

"You can talk normal and we'll hear you," Davis said. "No need for contortions."

"Right." I stiffened as something moved along the tree line. "I think she's coming." My cell phone rang. With trembling fingers, I pulled it from my pocket. "Hello?"

"Come toward me, CJ. I'm not stepping into the open like an idiot."

"Okay, I'm coming to the tree line opposite the restrooms."

Mae exhaled heavily. "Just hurry up."

Once I reached her, she yanked up my tee-shirt and ripped off the listening device. "You really need to be more subtle. The running commentary was a dead giveaway." She poked a gun into my side. "Start walking."

"Where?"

"Don't you want to see your loved ones?" She laughed and jabbed me again. "Pick up the pace. Do you have the ring?"

I shook my head. "I'll tell you where it is once my dog and Eric are free."

"So you want to play games. All right."

A shudder radiated up my spine as I recalled the nightmare of running through the woods. Mae even wore black like the faceless woman. "How far?"

"Not too far. A couple of miles. Walk fast, CJ. I don't want those cops getting too close."

"Where's Ioda and Myrna?"

"Sleeping like babies. Easy enough when helped with a sleeping pill."

I glanced over my shoulder, her features undistinguishable in the dark. "You've betrayed them."

"I wouldn't have had to if that stupid dog of yours hadn't alerted everyone to the stolen diamonds around the campground. But a woman has financial needs."

"Medical bills for your daughter?" I stumbled over an exposed tree root.

"You've done your homework. No, my little sweetie died before the age of eighteen. She slipped into a diabetic coma and into the arms of Jesus. I need this money to make a new life for myself in Mexico."

Not if I could help it. I wanted the woman behind bars. "You're a murderer."

"I didn't know that man couldn't swim." She jabbed me again and laughed. "Oh, you should have heard the uproar Myrna caused when she found out. Sweet idiot that she is. Can we stop talking now? I don't like eleventh-hour confessions."

"It passes the time." I scanned the ground

around me, searching through the inky blackness for a weapon. A creek babbled to our right. That meant there would be rocks. All I needed to do was get my hands on one. "I'm thirsty."

"Tough."

Where in the world was the cavalry? Ann would be devastated that Mae had gotten away with me.

"How can you tell where we're going?" I couldn't see a thing as evidenced by how many times I tripped.

"I've traveled this many times over the last few days. Just keep walking and stop talking."

"Talking keeps the bears away."

"It makes me irritable to hear you jabber on. You don't want to see what I'll do if I'm irritated."

Point taken. I clamped my mouth shut and stuck my hand in my pocket to make sure the ring was still there. It was. I wrapped my fingers around my bargaining chip.

An excited yipping. We were getting close to where Caper and Eric were held. My step quickened. The sooner I set eyes on them, the sooner this would all be over.

"Climb up."

I stared at the steep surface of a rock. "I'll slip."

"There are footholds. Feel for them." Another jab.

"Fine." I felt around until I found them and started to climb. The gym shoes I'd been smart enough to wear provided good traction, and I was staring into the dark mouth of a cave within a few minutes.

Mae turned on a lantern. "See? They're fine. I

told you I wasn't a murderer."

Eric narrowed his eyes and grunted.

Mae reached over and yanked the tape off. "I'm going to untie you and let the dog loose. Then I want CJ to give me what's mine."

I slipped my hand back into my pocket. "As soon as they are free and out of this cave."

"I won't leave you," Eric said.

"How touching." Mae cut the tape around his ankles, then his wrists. "Don't try anything or I'll shoot her. CJ, let the dog out, then the three of you stand against that wall."

She didn't have to tell me twice. I opened the cage and scooped Caper into my arms, then joined Eric against the wall of the cave.

"The ring, CJ."

I dug it from my pocket. Hopefully, by the time she figured out it was a fake, we'd be somewhere safe.

Mae grinned, her teeth flashing in the light of the lantern. "Now, we play. You didn't think I could let you two live, did you?" She tilted her head. "Give me the ring, then run."

Oh, God. It was the nightmare all over again. I tossed the ring out of the cave.

Eric grabbed my hand and dragged me outside. We slid down the rock face on our bottoms and dashed into the woods, Mae's obscenities following. I couldn't see a thing, but trusted Eric with all my heart.

"Do you know where you're going?" I asked.

"As far away from her as possible."

A gunshot rang out.

Caper yelped.

I pressed my lips together to stifle a scream. I couldn't alert Mae to our location.

"I'm going to enjoy killing you, CJ." For someone who said she didn't commit murder, Mae sure sounded like she wanted to kill me.

"Come on, sweetheart." Eric parted some low branches and pulled me through them and across a path as the first drops of rain fell. "Good. The rain will cover our tracks."

Oh, yeah? Eric wasn't in the last rainstorm where I'd run for my life. I squeezed his hand, glad for the assurance I wasn't alone this time. Whatever happened would happen with Eric by my side. I set Caper down to run along beside and give my arms a break from her squirming. Her four short legs would travel easier than my two.

"Where's Davis?" Eric stopped to let me catch my breath.

"I left him at my house. Ann should have been hiding in the bushes." Had something happened to her? "She said she wouldn't let me out of her sight."

"Then Mae must have gotten to her. Come on." We continued our trek through heavily wooded, uneven terrain, splashed through a creek, and up a steep hill. I might be tiny, but I was horribly out of shape. Still, sore muscles meant I still breathed.

"I see you," Mae sang. "I bet you wish you had night-vision goggles, too."

Eric growled. "Stay low. Make as small a target as possible. We have to reach your house."

I totally agreed. "Glad you know where you're going."

"I grew up in these woods." He held aside a branch for me. "Mae isn't as close as she wants us to believe. She may be able to see, but I know where the densest forest is. It'll be hard for her to get off a clear shot." A bullet kicked a chunk of bark off the tree near his head. "My mistake."

We barged like bulls through the woods, no longer caring about not making any noise. Our pursuer stayed close behind, firing off the occasional shot, and filling the air with laughter. She'd gone insane.

Eric stopped at the top of a cliff overlooking a wide creek. "Jump."

"What?" I yanked my hand free. "Caper?"

"She'll find her way. Go. It's deep enough. Jump and let the current carry you." He shoved me as another shot rang out.

I submerged, then broke water as he landed beside me. I reached out for him, grabbing his hand. Overhead, I saw Caper's head before clouds once again covered the moon. She ducked back. Eric was right. My little friend would find her way.

The swift-moving creek carried us away from a screaming Mae who promised to hunt us down if it took the rest of her days. Good luck with that, psycho.

The creek widened into a small pool, and Eric pulled me from the water before collapsing onto a patch of moss. He pressed a hand to his side. "She got me."

My mouth dried. "Is it bad?" I lifted his shirt, trying to see with no light. I probed with my fingers, bringing them away sticky. I didn't feel a hole, just a groove. "No penetration, but you'll need stitches. Let me take off your shirt and tie it around you."

I helped him out of the tee shirt, then tied it as tight around his middle as I could. "Can you make it home?"

"With that woman chasing us? You bet." He sprang to his feet. "We've gone the long way around, but we're not far from home now." He reclaimed my hand and we took off at a fast walk.

Finally, we broke free of the forest. I smiled at the sight of lights burning in the tiny houses of Heavenly Acres. We'd made it. We raced home and into my house to see the worry ease from the faces of our friends. My little house was packed with the people who cared about us.

Eric collapsed onto the sofa. "Mae is still out there and wanting revenge."

"Let me take a look at you." Amber knelt beside him. "I can stitch this, but you should go to the hospital."

"When this is over."

I glanced at Ann. "What happened?"

"She snuck up behind me and knocked me out. Davis found me lying there useless." Tears welled in her eyes. "I'm sorry, CJ."

"Don't feel bad. I'm here now." I placed a hand on her shoulder.

"She got the drop on me, too," Eric said. "Came right up behind me on the trail. The campfire was nothing more than a ruse."

"Did she tell you where Ioda and Myrna are?" Davis asked.

"Motel in town. Room 23." He hissed as Amber

poured disinfectant on his graze. "She knocked them out with drugs."

Davis placed a call to Milton, telling him where he could pick up the other two thieves.

I turned as the door swung open.

Mae stood there with a gun aimed at my heart.

Before Mae could pull the trigger, Mags stepped up behind her and zapped her with her Taser. Mae fell, still training her gun on me.

Ann fired and struck the other woman in the leg. My bodyguard had managed to save me after all.

Caper bounded up the steps and clamped her teeth around Mae's gun hand. Growling, she shook her head.

I stepped forward and kicked the gun out of her reach before seizing my dog. "You'll get to start a new life after all." I grinned down at her.

She snarled up at me. "I should have shot you right off."

"But then we couldn't have played." I kept a firm grip on my dog and sat next to Eric.

When Amber finished with him, she put a bandage around Mae's thigh. "The hospital can finish with you. All I'll do is keep you from bleeding to death."

Sirens wailed in the distance.

"When I saw this no-good woman sneaking up your porch, I called an ambulance. I knew one way or the other she'd need medical attention." Mags grinned, slipping her Taser into the pocket of her fuzzy pink robe. "I know everyone makes fun of me being the neighborhood Nosy Nellie, but it comes in handy, don't you think?"

I wrapped my arms around her in a hug. "You're an amazing woman, and I'm lucky to call you friend."

Chapter Twenty-two

The next morning, we gathered around the picnic table and enjoyed a breakfast of pancakes cooked by Mags. Eric moved stiffly with stitches in his side, but still managed to put away quite a stack.

Davis told us between bites about the arrest of the three women. "Ioda and Myrna were sleeping like the dead. Didn't even wake up when Milton entered their room. He thought at first Mae might have given them too much of that sleeping pill, but they woke up fast enough when he slapped the handcuffs on them."

"Did they have any idea that Carol, I mean, Mae, was double-crossing them?" I forked another pancake from the pile in the middle of the table onto my plate.

"No idea, but they were plenty mad when they found out." He grinned. "Another job well done." He glanced at Ann. "You're a good cop."

Her face reddened. "I got hit from behind."

"Happens to the best of us." He wiped his mouth with a napkin. "Ranger here got caught, too, and he knows every inch of this mountain."

Eric chuckled. "Don't remind me. Made me feel like a greenhorn." He rubbed his mouth. "Still hurts where she yanked off the tape."

"I can't wait to see what happens next," Mags said. "Life hasn't been boring since CJ took this job."

Eric put an arm around my shoulders and pulled me close. "It sure hasn't." He placed his lips on mine. "But a few months of boredom might be nice."

I couldn't agree more and kissed him again. "I'll do my best to stay out of trouble, if Caper can do the same." Hearing her name, Caper leaned her paws on my leg. I fed her a piece of pancake. I didn't think Caper's and my adventures would stop anytime soon.

"You mean I might get a second chance at keeping CJ safe?" Ann wiggled her eyebrows. "Sweet. I'll watch my back next time."

The good-natured ribbing continued through breakfast, but while I loved my friends, I wanted time alone with my man. The others left, and Eric led me to our spot, the fallen log on the shore of the lake.

We sat shoulder to shoulder and watched the morning sun glimmer across the mirror-like surface. "Thank you," I said.

"For what?" He smiled down at me.

"Not dying at the hands of Mae. When I saw the photo of you tied up, I was afraid that was the last thing I'd see of you." I raised tear-filled eyes to his face.

"Sweetheart, you can't get rid of me that easy." He gave me another of his deep kisses that made me forget everything but him…

…until the Next Adventure.

Check out the next book, Caper Finds a Clue, by scanning this code.

SCAN ME

Dear Reader,

I hope you're having as much fun with this cast of characters as I am and are looking forward to the next book in the series, titled *Caper Finds a Clue*. If you've enjoyed *Caper Goes Missing*, please leave a review. Reviews are invaluable to an author.

God bless,
Cynthia Hickey

If you missed the first book in the series, *No Small Caper*, you can get it on Amazon.

Website at www.cynthiahickey.com

Multi-published and Amazon and ECPA Best-Selling author Cynthia Hickey has sold close to a million copies of her works since 2013. She has taught a Continuing Education class at the 2015 American Christian Fiction Writers conference, several small ACFW chapters and RWA chapters, and small writer retreats. She and her husband run the small press, Winged Publications, which includes some of the CBA's best well-known authors. She lives in Arizona and Arkansas, becoming a snowbird, with her husband and one dog. She has nine grandchildren who keep her busy and tell everyone they know that "Nana is a writer".

Connect with me on FaceBook
Twitter
Bookbub
Sign up for my newsletter and receive a free short story
www.cynthiahickey.com

Follow me on Amazon

Enjoy other books by Cynthia Hickey

Fantasy (written as Cynthia Melton)
Fate of the Faes
Shayna

Deema
Kasdeya

Time Travel
The Portal

Tiny House Mysteries
No Small Caper

A Hollywood Murder
Killer Pose, book 1
Killer Snapshot, book 2
Shoot to Kill, book 3
Kodak Kill Shot, book 4
To Snap a Killer

Shady Acres Mysteries
Beware the Orchids, book 1
Path to Nowhere
Poison Foliage
Poinsettia Madness
Deadly Greenhouse Gases
Vine Entrapment

CLEAN BUT GRITTY

Highland Springs

Murder Live
Say Bye to Mommy
To Breathe Again

Colors of Evil Series

Shades of Crimson
Coral Shadows

The Pretty Must Die Series

Ripped in Red, book 1
Pierced in Pink, book 2
Wounded in White, book 3
Worthy, The Complete Story

Lisa Paxton Mystery Series

Eenie Meenie Miny Mo
Jack Be Nimble
Hickory Dickory Dock

One Hour (A short story thriller)

INSPIRATIONAL
(scroll down to see clean books without inspirational
message)

Whisper Sweet Nothings (a short romance)

Nosy Neighbor Series
Anything For A Mystery, Book 1
A Killer Plot, Book 2
Skin Care Can Be Murder, Book 3

Death By Baking, Book 4
Jogging Is Bad For Your Health, Book 5
Poison Bubbles, Book 6
A Good Party Can Kill You, Book 7 (Final)
Nosy Neighbor collection

Christmas with Stormi Nelson

The Summer Meadows Series
Fudge-Laced Felonies, Book 1
Candy-Coated Secrets, Book 2
Chocolate-Covered Crime, Book 3
Maui Macadamia Madness, Book 4
All four novels in one collection

The River Valley Mystery Series
Deadly Neighbors, Book 1
Advance Notice, Book 2
The Librarian's Last Chapter, Book 3
All three novels in one collection

Historical cozy
Hazel's Quest

Historical Romances
Runaway Sue
Taming the Sheriff
Sweet Apple Blossom
A Doctor's Agreement
A Lady Maid's Honor

A Touch of Sugar
Love Over Par
Heart of the Emerald

Finding Love the Harvey Girl Way
Cooking With Love
Guiding With Love
Serving With Love
Warring With Love
All 4 in 1

A Wild Horse Pass Novel
They Call Her Mrs. Sheriff, book 1 (A Western
Romance)

Finding Love in Disaster
The Rancher's Dilemma
The Teacher's Rescue
The Soldier's Redemption

Woman of courage Series

A Love For Delicious
Ruth's Redemption
Charity's Gold Rush
Mountain Redemption
Woman of Courage series (all four books)

Short Story Westerns
Desert Rose
Desert Lilly
Desert Belle

Desert Daisy
Flowers of the Desert 4 in 1

Romantic Suspense

Overcoming Evil series
Mistaken Assassin
Captured Innocence
Mountain of Fear
Exposure at Sea
A Secret to Die for
Collision Course
Romantic Suspense of 5 books in 1

The Game
Suspicious Minds
After the Storm
Local Betrayal

Contemporary

Romance in Paradise
Maui Magic
Sunset Kisses
Deep Sea Love
3 in 1

Finding a Way Home
Service of Love
Hillbilly Cinderella
Unraveling Love
I'd Rather Kiss My Horse

Christmas

Romancing the Fabulous Cooper Brothers
Handcarved Christmas
The Payback Bride
Curtain Calls and Christmas Wishes
Christmas Gold
A Christmas Stamp
Snowflake Kisses
A Christmas Deception

The Red Hat's Club (Contemporary novellas)

Finally
Suddenly
Surprisingly
The Red Hat's Club 3 – in 1

Short Story

One Hour (A short story thriller)
Whisper Sweet Nothings (a Valentine short romance)